A Great Silence Universe Novel
THE SIGNAL
The Signal Series: Book Two
I0748743
Meredith McCray

The Signal
by Meredith McCray

For permission requests, contact:
meredith_mccray_author@proton.me

Edited by Calliope Pemberton
Cover design and illustrations by Hydrangea Design Co.

First edition, 2026.
ISBN: 979-8-9944851-2-5

✦ ✦ ✦

"Sometimes even to live is an act of courage."
— Lucius Annaeus Seneca

✦ ✦ ✦

Contents

Prologue

The planet had been silent for years, but today the quiet felt dangerous.

Even the wind had gone still.

Doc stood at the edge of the observation platform, staring into the white where storm and horizon had long ago stopped pretending to be separate things. The surface of Honora had been stripped down to motion, cold, and force. Nothing lived there. Nothing moved unless it was driven.

Below her, the tunnels held.

They always held.

For now.

She heard it then.

Not the familiar groan of the structure settling against the cold. Not the thin whistle of air through an imperfect seam. Something sharper than that. Smaller. Irregular enough to catch in the ear.

She turned her head and listened.

There it was again.

A cry.

Then another.

Doc did not move at first. She stood very still, as if the sound might correct itself if she waited long enough. As if the world might decide it had made a mistake and quietly undo it before she had to witness the proof.

It didn't.

She crossed the platform quickly and descended into the medical shelter, following the sound through the narrow corridors where the air always smelled faintly of stone, machine oil, and cold metal.

The door was already open.

She did not remember leaving it that way.

Inside, the room was warmer than the rest of the complex, heat dragged from systems that could not really afford to spare it. Emergency cradles lined the wall.

Every one of them were occupied.

Doc stopped in the doorway.

There were seven. It was not expected, not really even possible.

And still—there they were.

Moving. Crying. Alive.

A baby's cry can pierce even the thickest walls. It is one of the few sounds desperate enough to carry through steel and stone as though neither were there at all.

Doc crossed the room and went to work.

She checked the nearest cradle first.

Breathing.

Stable.

The next.

Warm enough.

The next.

Heart rate elevated, but strong.

She moved from one infant to another with practiced hands and a mind that refused, for the moment, to ask any question it could not survive answering.

Seven.

No mothers present, only names as their record. No explanation she trusted enough to shape into words. There were more immediate things to do.

They grew.

Not evenly, not quietly, and never predictably enough to make Doc comfortable, but steadily enough that the days arranged themselves around hunger, fever, sleep, tears, and the thousand small emergencies of keeping fragile things alive in a place never meant to hold them.

She gave them names of significance known only to her.

Lio. Thia. Rosa.

And the others.

Seven, always.

She kept count in her head, because the systems did not always record correctly anymore. Sometimes numbers shifted when she was not looking. Sometimes a log would show a result she knew she had not entered. Sometimes equipment behaved as though it had briefly forgotten what it was for.

She stopped relying on the machines where she could.

The children learned quickly.

Too quickly, in some ways.

Not in language or numbers or reading. Those came easily enough. The books in the science complex became treasures to them, and reading, mercifully, was one of the few quiet things seven brilliant children could do at once. Doc turned numbers into games, coding into puzzles, ethics into stories, and made education feel as much like play as she could manage.

Children were meant to learn through wonder.

Even here.

Especially here.

She did not teach them everything.

Not because she wanted to keep them small, but because knowledge was weight, and she had to be careful what she asked their young minds to carry.

They called her Doc.

Not because she had asked them to.

Because once, long ago, one of the youngest had reached for her in the dim light and called her something else.

Mother.

Doc had gone still.

Then, gently, she shook her head.

"No," she had said softly.

The child had blinked up at her. "Why?"

Doc had not answered right away. She had adjusted the blanket around their shoulders instead, checked their breathing with the same absent tenderness she gave everything she was trying too hard not to love.

"Because that belongs to someone else," she said at last.

The child had considered that with the solemn gravity only children can bring to something they do not understand.

Then they nodded.

"Doc," they said again, trying the shape of it.

Doc nodded back.

That was enough.

It had to be.

The transmitter still functioned.

Barely.

Doc kept it alive anyway.

It had been built for a different world. One where a signal sent outward might still matter by the time it arrived. One where help, if it came at all, might come in something smaller than years.

Still, she maintained it.

Out of habit.

Out of duty.

Out of something lonelier she preferred not to examine too closely.

The message itself never changed.

It had never needed to.

Simple enough to remember.

Simple enough to repeat.

Simple enough to become ritual.

She was teaching them something she did not want them to learn.

But something she believed they might one day need more than anything else.

A thing to send into silence, not because silence was expected to answer, but because saying it felt like a refusal to disappear completely.

At first the children treated it like a game. Then a task. Then something quieter and more serious.

Doc never named that either.

One of them listened differently.

Reve.

Doc noticed it early and, at first, made the mistake of telling herself it was harmless.

Reve lingered where the others passed through. Paused where the others kept moving. Pressed her small hand against the walls as though she expected something to answer from the other side.

When the floor trembled, Reve would crouch and lay her palm against it, listening to the vibration as if it held language she nearly understood. When the humming started in the deeper parts of the facility, she would stop and turn toward it, still as a compass needle.

Sometimes Doc would catch her staring at a wall as though she were looking through it into the next room.

"Stay with the others," Doc told her once.

Reve looked crestfallen. She never argued, but she also never stopped.

Doc considered separating her. Redirecting her attention. Keeping her close enough that whatever strange pull had settled into the child would have less room to deepen.

She did not.

Not because she believed it was safe.

Because Doc did not yet understand what danger looked like for them. And because there were things the body could recover from that the mind could not.

The storms worsened.

Outer sensors failed in pieces. Power had to be shifted by hand more often than not. Heat became something negotiated from room to room. The tunnels held, though not always in the same way and never as reassuringly as before.

Still, the children adapted.

Children always do.

They became people in a place that had not been made for people. They learned which corridors stayed warm longest, which doors stuck in the cold, which sounds mattered, and which only frightened you if you listened too hard.

As part of their day, Doc let them roam.

Not unwatched because she was careless, but because one day she would be gone and they would have only each other. They needed freedom as much as caution. They needed play as much as survival.

So she gave them rules instead of walls.

Stay together.

Avoid the sealed doors.

Come back before dark cycle.

They always came back.

Cold. Hungry. Occasionally hurt.

But back.

Until one night they didn't.

In the morning, there were six.

Doc knew it before she counted. Some absences arrive fully formed, unmistakable before the mind has agreed to admit them.

Still, she checked.

Storage rooms.

Outer corridors.

The narrow connecting passages where heat pooled strangely and vanished without warning.

She called once.

Then not again.

Sound traveled badly now. Sometimes too far. Sometimes nowhere useful at all.

She found nothing.

No blood.

No torn fabric.

No body.

No failure she could isolate and repair.

Just absence.

Reve was gone.

When Doc returned to the main chamber, the others were waiting for her. Watching her face with the terrible stillness children wear when they already know the answer and need you to say something anyway.

Doc did not say the number aloud.

She would not make it more real than it already was.

One of them began to cry.

The sound split the room.

Doc crossed to them without thinking and gathered them close, holding the nearest child against her chest while the others folded in by instinct, grief making a single frightened shape of them all.

She could not fix it.

She could only refuse to let them stand in it alone.

When the crying finally quieted, she stepped back and made herself into something steadier than she felt.

"We stay together now," she said.

A rule.

Not an explanation.

The children nodded.

They always nodded.

Above them, the wind screamed across Honora's frozen surface.

Below, in the last warm room on the planet, six children huddled close to the failing transmitter while its message continued its long journey into the dark.

Weak.

Failing.

Still alive.

One of the children stood beside Doc and asked, in a voice gone thin with exhaustion, "Who will hear it?"

Doc looked at the display.

At the pattern repeating itself into distance.

At the silence that followed.

She did not know whether the question still meant what it once had, or if anyone had ever truly been close enough to answer.

She reached down and pulled the remaining twin gently against her side, smoothing a hand over their hair with a tenderness she no longer bothered trying to hide.

“Someone,” she said.

And watched as the message was sent again.

Chapter 1

Lieutenant Commander Jo Willis sat at attention, prepared to report on the Signal. She waited to speak seated across from Epsilon Station Commander Buck Rogers. His stateroom was grand for one that never received visitors. The table was polished regularly and reflected light from an ancient-looking chandelier. Maps of Terra and portraits of her former leaders adorned the walls in gilded frames.

Lieutenant Horace Simmons and Lieutenant Janelle Keller were also present to give their account of events. Her subordinates had presented their reports already. The three of them had direct knowledge of and worked on Terra's first known Signal Contact. The news of unexpected contact reverberated through the station.

Commander Rogers started her off with an easy question. "Comm officer Keller reported that the Signal is in Terran. Security officer

Simmons reported the nature of the message to be a distress call. What else can you tell us about the Signal Science officer Willis?"

She rehearsed this part many times. Jo wanted to get it just right for the record—swapping emphasis on some parts, leaving some out entirely. No one needed to hear about dreams, and she couldn't explain them anyway. Taking a breath, she clasped her hands together under the table.

"The Signal is very old." Jo animatedly recounted the various theories and historical methods she tested using a book she found in the science library. She nearly rushed through how the work led to the Signal revealing itself. Rogers offered no encouragement and looked at her impassively. The code they intercepted was not of alien origin. Squeezing her hands tightly, she braced herself for what she was about to reveal.

"The only possible explanation is that people of Terran-origin created the Signal."

Jo stopped talking.

There would be questions.

Instead, the officers exchanged uneasy glances—Jo had kept that last part to herself these past few weeks.

Rogers added a note on his datapad. Keller angled herself straighter—she didn't appreciate her friend keeping this information secret.

“Terran-origin? Care to explain that?” The commander was not trying to interrogate her, but he also wasn’t having a conversation either.

Jo had prepared for this question with additional research in her free time, spending significant amounts of it in the science library.

“Many theories predicting the end of The Great Silence have been considered over the centuries. None of them ever prepared us for a result like this. That our first contact would be with people from our own system. The sentinel stations were designed to look for deep space signals of *extraterrestrial* origin.” The group hung on her every word.

“I was intrigued that a signal could be received intact, while also being old in both origin and technique. It’s not something that should be possible.” Jo was tempted to pause again but she pressed on, excited to share the findings.

“What I discovered was also something that I didn’t know was possible. Terran colonies existed before The Healing.”

For a long time it felt like no one in the room breathed. Jo dug her fingernails into the palms of her hands. She had to let them respond before piling on any new information.

The idea of colonies that technically didn't exist left her wanting more. The commander looked uncomfortable. Surely operational and tactical intel like that would not be suppressed. He made another note on the datapad, and pressed save more forcefully than intended.

"Colonies? *Terran* Colonies?" Keller was the first to speak. "Why didn't we know about them?" She began to talk rapidly. "They wouldn't just leave them there... right?" She sounded more upset than curious. As the tone in the room shifted from procedure to emotion, Jo suggested they break for a while.

The commander agreed and said there was bound to be more they had to answer for. That turned out to be more accurate than he realized.

On Tau Station, the androids were focused on the Signal in their own ways. Some not taking any interest at all, and others wanting to work the problem.

Sam paced in her quarters, repeating the Signal message.

“Please send help. Please, send help. Please... Send... Help."

No matter how she tried to add intonation, it didn't help create more meaning for her. "That’s all they said, Sensor." She turned away from the bookcase where her pacing route ended, and turned to him. She paced some more, taking a circular route around the common room table.

"Why not more information? Who are they? Where are they? What kind of help?”

Her pacing and talking speed quickened in tandem. Sensor was worried about Sam. She spent her whole life isolated on the lower decks with only algae to tend to. He theorized those conditions may have heightened her sensitivity to strained systems.

“Would you like to catalogue your queries, then we could systematically attempt to understand and resolve them?”

Sam stopped pacing and spun around to face him.

“We?” She said searching his face for signs of an expression.

"I am attempting to indicate I will work with you on this important mission." A slow smile spread on his face. Of course Sam knew what he meant. He often used literal humor to settle her nervousness. He brought the rolling chair from her terminal over the table, giving her a way to be still and move at the same time. She rolled around the table and continued talking.

"I would like to catalogue my important queries with you."

Chapter 2

The science library on the station had become a gathering place since Jo found the "secret" to the Signal. Residents gained interest in physical books, hoping to find a secret of their own.

She was giving a presentation to her crew in continued pursuit of the senders of the mysterious message. But the star charts were in the science library and there wasn't room to spread out, so she resorted to old methods of interoffice communications.

"Based on these star charts, the most likely planet to house our missing colony is here." "Most likely?" Simmons pressed.Jo continued on, "The Signal's origin isn't drifting. It's fixed. I mapped it against surviving expansion records—what little we have. There were only a handful of colonies ever projected that far out."She zoomed the display. "This is the only match that holds."

The pair of officers squinted and leaned forward in their seats trying to identify the tiny speck on the screen. "Oh, sorry about that," Jo saw her mistake and zoomed in on the projection, "this one." She was not used to working on small screens and connection lag between rooms.

"Well, what is it?" Simmons was invigorated by being part of the exclusive group. He had been more engaged than Jo could ever recall.

"The planet is named Honora. The location for the colony was initially chosen for its position at the outer edge of the habitable zone."

"Those poor people," Keller said with a faraway tone. "I still just don't understand how we could lose a whole colony!" She had gone through several stages of grief over a group of people she never knew existed. Jo didn't want to talk about feelings, she just wanted to get to work.

Jo had walked them through the Healing and the loss of Terra's academic and scientific knowledge. After the universities were rebuilt, and lost texts reclaimed, no complete records of the Terran colonies were ever recovered. As far as anyone knew, they simply didn't exist anymore.

Keller had struggled with this more than the others. Overall sentiment on the station was cheerful, finding a message from a long-lost colony was good news. She seemed fixated on the loss, while Jo and the others were trying to move forward with planning.

✦ ✦ ✦

"So we know where they are, and what they said, but what are we supposed to do about it?"

Jo hesitated.

"We help them Ace, what else is there to do?" in Keller's distress she subconsciously used his nickname.

"Jan," he said, exhaling. "It's not that I don't think we *shouldn't* help. Just that I don't know what our help would actually entail." He became defensive with the group sentiment not on his side.

From separate rooms, the women each opened their mouths to reply and then closed them again. A dejected Keller sat back from the table with her hands in her lap. She hung her head, looking at her fingernails. Simmons pretended to reinspect the star chart on the screen, hoping to let the tense moment pass.

From the science library, Jo scrunched her face and blew out a hard breath. "We don't decide."

"What?" Keller and Simmons exclaimed in unison.

Jo turned the projection off, and her camera on—while she was the mission commander, she wasn't the station commander.

"We do not need to decide this," gesturing to the three of them. "Especially not right now. The Signal and call for help is significantly larger than us. I will speak to Commander Rogers, and we will reconvene after I receive his recommendation."

Simmons curled his lip at the deferral, while Keller released a breath she was holding. Jo watched them both, uneasy.

✦ ✦ ✦

Deep in the belly of Tau Station, Chip, Najma, Sam and Sensor gathered in Sam's quarters. The invitation had been mysterious, but they came happily. Visiting each other's quarters was still a novelty they enjoyed whenever possible.

There was an air of conspiracy as Sam had purposely left Indarra out of the conversation. He had a tendency to take over and interrupt thoughtful discussions—what she wanted to discuss would take focus. Chip and Sensor sat together at the main table.

Milling about, Najma stood admiring Sam's bookcase. It was once empty and was now brimming with an assortment of things she'd never seen before. The shelves were filled with molecular models, photos of algae, and an especially colorful diagram of something called the Krebs Cycle. She'd ask about the significance of the latter one another time.

"Is it ok to touch this one, Sam?" Najma motioned to a ball and stick model on the shelf at their eye level. She thought it looked kind of like a comet with a large body and long tail.

"Yes, and please be mindful of the tail—it's fallen off a couple times already. The hydrocarbon chain is kind of weak." Sam made a slight grimace to herself, knowing Sensor created the model for her. She didn't want to offend his craft.

"Perhaps I will just observe it from here. What... is it?"

"Oh, I am glad you asked!" Sam clapped her hands several times, a mannerism that brought her great joy lately. "This molecule is called chlorophyll. It is an essential part of algae's chemical metabolism. It is responsible for converting light into energy." Sam loved to talk about algae.

"Any other interesting facts about this one?" Sensor inquired. He was attempting to take social pressure off of Najma by asking. He knew the answer already, Sam had given him many lectures on chlorophyll in their days together.

Sam turned to give him a quizzical look, but grinned when she saw him incline his head in Najma's direction.

"There definitely are many more remarkable aspects to this molecule. My favorite being is that it is also a pigment that gives algae its green color." Namja tilted her head at this new information.

"But your figure is not green. It's several different colors, none of them are green." Sam furrowed her brow not getting the connection.

Sensor swooped in to answer her comment.

"Perhaps if Sam would like, I could create a green version the next time the tail on this one falls off." He heard her clap a little more just then.

From the back of the room, Chip simulated a yawn and stretch, feeling ignored by his friends.

"Well this has been very boring. Why did you ask us to come here?" The *you* in question being Sam and Sensor. He thought they were one more shift away from combining their quarters, they spent so much free time together. Maybe he was just missing spending time with his friend.

Sensor did an exaggerated eyeroll at him, showing he understood the comment to be sarcastic. All the androids on the station had taken to trying human mannerisms, though they did not seem to serve a purpose.

Sam walked over to the table and sat down, while activating a handheld screen. She brought up an image of the station with an illustration of a beam coming at it. Najma and Chip looked at the screen, then each other, and then back at Sam and Sensor.

"Well," she said, taking her time, "I was hoping you'd help us find out where the Signal came from."

CHAPTER 3

Walking from the science library to the bridge deck wasn't arduous, but people kept stopping Jo to ask her questions or greet her. She wasn't particularly happy to be a celebrity. She didn't do anything special, just her job. Rogers reminded her that she was a role model and to be gracious to station inhabitants, they were all each other had.

Jo was about to enter the commander's private office, but stopped, seeing Evan Chen standing in front of his door. Whether he was debating to go in, or was being made to wait outside, she couldn't say. Clearing her throat, so as not to startle him, she stood next to her friend and faced the door as well. She rocked back on her heels, he didn't react.

"Didn't expect to see you here. Couldn't sleep?" She playfully tagged him on the arm. It was intended as friendly banter, but looking up at him, the man seemed disheveled and exhausted. His face was thinner than usual. "Hey," she said gently, and placed a hand lightly on his arm, Chen finally looked down at her. His eyes were clouded with dark circles beneath them. What was he doing out here? "Come with me," she guided him away from the door, tucking one arm under his and the other around his waist. She didn't know where she was taking him yet.

Without protest, Chen allowed her to lead him from the door, walking with her in a daze. Choosing privacy and comfort, she decided to go back to her quarters.

Jo was carefully holding Chen around the waist, guiding him through the halls. She approached the lift. As she did, Keller and Simmons stumbled out laughing. Jo was glad to see them, but didn't stop to talk. Keller gave her an inquisitive, but alarmed look, as if to say, "is he okay?" Jo shook her head slowly, eyes exaggeratedly wide. She mouthed, "don't ask," and kept walking with Chen into the lift and pressed the level for the officer's quarters. They made it from the lift to her quarters with no one else noticing.

Turning the lights on a comfortable setting in her living area, she sat Chen on a couch and brought him a blanket. He nearly snatched it out of her hands before bundling up in it. Jo took a deep breath. *What did I get myself into?* She made some warm citrus tea with honey-flavored syrup. His favorite. She didn't care for tea, but made herself a cup anyway.

Once their beverages were ready, she sat opposite him in a chair shaped like a precariously placed bowl. She sat with him in silence, sipping the mildly astringent tea.

"I had a nightmare," Chen stared past her clutching the tea. He adjusted his shoulders like he was uncomfortable, trying to reposition the blanket.

"Oh?" Jo said, the word breathed over the steam of her cup.

"I was in a frozen room," he continued unmoving. Jo's blood ran cold. She stilled in her seated position. Her dream of a similar room chilled her, and now, someone else.

"Everything was covered in ice. Really thick, hard ice. But I didn't feel cold." Jo focused intensely on his recounting of the dream. Her eyes narrowed and she clutched the mug tighter in her hands. She barely breathed,

"There was a lot of laboratory equipment scattered around the tables and floors."

She let out a breath she didn't realize she was holding. *Maybe it's not the same as mine,* she thought. Chen continued his description, eyes not focused on anything, and pulled the blanket even closer.

"I tried inspecting the shelves on the wall. But before I could see what was on them, I heard a terrible and loud cry." Jo's heart started racing, and her breath went shallow. He continued not noticing her reaction, "I couldn't figure out where it was coming from. It felt like it was everywhere—"

"Did you find the door?" Jo blurted and then clapped a hand over her mouth. Eyes wide, Chen snapped back into the present at her comment. He adjusted his position on the couch, getting more comfortable from when he plopped down unaware. He looked at her for a moment, then away."There was a bar covering it. I got it open but it was too dark." He shook his head a fraction, "I woke up before anything else happened." He looked down at his cup and shivered. The memory of the dream chilled hi m.Looking down at her tea, Jo said softly, "it was stairs. In my dream, there were stairs behind the door. I tried going down them."

"What happened?" Chen asked, visibly shaken at this development. How could they--her words interrupting his thoughts.

"Something stopped me. A hand." His eyebrows furrowed at the development.

"Who?" he asked breathlessly.

"Not a who," Jo said, "a what. It was an android hand." She shuddered, feeling like she needed a blanket too. Chen, seeing her reaction, tossed her the knit blanket that was beside him on the couch. She gratefully caught it and wrapped herself in it. A corner of the fabric fell in her tea, but she didn't care.

Evan looked at her earnestly, "What do you think it means?" She looked away, lost in thought, and wrapped the blanket tighter around her shoulders.

Shrugging, instead of answering, Jo stared blankly at the wall.

Chapter 4

The android leaders of Tau Station gathered in the multipurpose bay on the communications deck. They recently completed renovations. The bay now carried an air of formality that was new to them. A round table, chairs, and interactive screens were arranged on the sides of the room. The new space made their leadership body feel official.

During the room design phase, they considered opinions from all of the androids on what to include. Having opinions to share was new in itself—their progression to individuality had been steadily growing. Indarra wanted an oblong table so he could sit at one end, but Sam did not agree with him. She said they all had an equal stake in ensuring the station ran well, so none should be set apart from the others. The logic satisfied the group. The security lead simulated a huff and crossed his arms across his chestplate, displeased at not getting his way. Sam just wanted a place where they could talk about the station without everyone's voice echoing off the walls.

Najma was chosen to deliver the news. She tensed for a moment, then relaxed, unsure how this would be received.

"In an effort to better understand the Signal, its message, as well as origination," she paused imperceptibly and glanced at Sam, who motioned for her to continue. "A subset of this group took action to determine the location of the Signal."

The room erupted.

"Why would we—" was one of the few phrases she could pick out.

"Is that truly wise?" Square had the last word.

The four exchanged a glance. Wisdom had not been part of their plan. Chip and Najma looked to Sam to take the lead, but she did not move. Sensor frowned at her unusually long pause.

Sam blinked and launched into her reply, "We were curious about the plea, and if location was... out of reach. The decision to not bring this to a vote was entirely mine." Sensor's eyebrows knitted together, adding consternation to his frown. Chip and Najma looked at each other in confusion. While she wasn't lying, Sam wasn't being truthful either. A conversation to bring a vote simply had not happened. "When I approached the others to help locate the Signal source, I was not sure we would find it—or not find it quickly."

Some at the table grumbled that this was acceptable but not satisfactory, while others murmured approval at their restraint.

"Were you successful in your endeavor?" Square said with an air of authority that was new and unsettling to Sam. Her mouth twitched slightly.

Najma straightened her posture and replied with stoic determination. "Yes."

The table erupted again. Some popped up from their seats, others throwing their hands up in the air. It was as though they were mimicking old Terran programs about how people acted in an office.

"When—"

"How long—"

"—what are we going to do—"

Sam took that as her cue, "we brought the information to this body because the location was determined. Now we have to decide what to do about it." She did not offer more explanation. The group settled down into a restless quiet, attempting to absorb this information more fully.

Unsatisfied with the brevity, Square again took the lead, "why don't you start by telling us what you found."

The four looked at each other again, none wanting to be the one to speak this time.

✦ ✦ ✦

While Tau Station argued about whether intervention was possible, the Terrans had already decided how the plan would unfold.

The Epsilon observation deck lights were dimmed to reduce glare from the starfield beyond the glass. The system containing Honora glowed faintly on the projection in the center of the table they had gathered around.

It was nothing but talking for nearly half an hour. Or circling.

Keller had her elbows on the table, hands wrapped around a mug she had forgotten to drink from. Jo stood near the projection instead of sitting, arms folded.

Simmons watched them all for a moment before speaking.

"We're not defining the mission."

The room went quiet.

Jo turned toward him. "Explain."

Simmons leaned forward, resting his forearms on the table. "We keep saying we're going to *help them.*" He gestured toward the star map. "That's not a mission."

Jo raised an eyebrow. "Seems pretty straightforward."

"No," Simmons said calmly. "It's vague."

He tapped the table once at the edge of the projection. "What we are planning is a search and rescue operation."

Keller shook her head silently. "They aren't lost."

"They sent a distress call," Simmons replied. "That qualifies."

He reached over and expanded the projection. Honora's orbit appeared, a faint ring near the outer edge of the habitable band. "Step one: search." He pointed at the planet. "We locate the colony—that alone could take a significant amount of time. Confirm population size. Evaluate environmental stability and infrastructure."

Jo stilled, considering the list. Although no one had said it out loud, they didn't truly know where the colony was on the planet.

"Step two: rescue." He leaned back in his chair. "We stabilize whatever systems are failing. Provide medical care. Supply shortages. Communication restoration."

Keller exhaled quietly. "I like it."

Simmons didn't react.

"Step three," he continued, "is relocation."

The word hung in the air.

Keller froze.

"Relocation?"

Simmons nodded confidently. "They're living on a failing frontier colony at the edge of the habitable zone. The infrastructure is centuries old. Their population is likely extremely small." He gestured toward the projection again. "That is not a sustainable environment."

Jo crossed her arms tighter.

"You're proposing evacuation."

"I'm describing the logical conclusion of the rescue mission."

Keller stared at the map.

"You think they'll leave?"

Simmons didn't hesitate.

"Of course they will."

The certainty in his voice settled over the table.

"They sent a *distress call*," he continued, hating to repeat himself. "If someone asks for help under these conditions, they expect extraction."

Jo studied the star map for a long moment. She had decided without speaking.

Keller still looked uneasy, but she didn't argue.

Simmons leaned back in his chair again, satisfied.

Beyond the glass, Honora's faint star burned quietly in the projection.

CHAPTER 5

Sam was behaving illogically.

Sensor recognized the pattern quickly, but he could not determine the cause. He observed her work through several off-shift cycles. When her scheduled tasks ended, she frequently diverted to the algae farms instead of returning to their quarters. The detour was not recorded in any task log.

She had developed a preference for vat room seven.

Temperature: stable. Light spectrum: consistent. Nutrient flow: within acceptable variance.

He verified the parameters twice. Nothing distinguished vat room seven from the others. Yet Sam remained there. Sometimes she stood between the vats, looking into the green suspension as if waiting for it to change.

It never did.

Other times she sat at the terminal reviewing the growth reports. The data did not vary between inspections. Still she scrolled through the records repeatedly, moving up and down the same sequences of measurements. He watched the screen once while standing behind her.

The numbers did not change.

Sam shook her head once, sharply, as if attempting to dislodge a thought that would not resolve. Sensor stepped back to avoid interfering with her work. Several times she tapped the display with her fingertip.

The terminal was not haptic. No response occurred. Sam did not appear to notice.

During these visits she sometimes became completely still.

The first time this happened Sensor assumed she was processing a complex computation. But the pauses repeated. Fractions of a second. Never long enough to trigger a system alert.

Stillness.

Then motion resumed as if nothing had happened. He started to measuring them.

0.32 seconds, 0.41 seconds, 0.29 seconds

The interruptions did not correspond to any internal processing cycle he could identify.

Sam never acknowledged them. She continued scrolling through the algae reports as though searching for something.

Sensor could not determine what.

On the sixth observation cycle he moved closer. Sam did not react to his presence.

Her gaze remained fixed on the algae vats. The suspension moved slowly within the glass cylinders, drifting in quiet spirals under the station lights.

Sensor initially assumed Sam was studying their behavior in response to stress. He checked the algae first. Then he checked the readouts. Nothing unusual.

Sam watched them as if waiting for something to reveal itself.

She leaned forward—then froze.

0.38 seconds.

When she moved again, she exhaled softly—another Terran mannerism.

Sensor waited.

Sam returned to the terminal and resumed scrolling through the reports.

Nothing had changed.

Sensor stood beside her for several minutes. He did not interrupt.

Eventually Sam closed the display and looked back into the vats.

"Everything is functioning normally," she said quietly.

The statement was accurate, but he experienced an unfamiliar uncertainty.

He should have recorded it. He didn't.

If everything was normal—why did it feel otherwise?

CHAPTER 6

Jo stood by her chair at Commander Rogers' conference table, the harsh light hurting her eyes. She scanned the maps on the walls idly as the commander walked in.

"How can I help, Lieutenant Commander?" He asked while taking his seat opposite her.

Jo bit the inside of her cheek lightly, she called the meeting to ask for a favor and did not feel confident it would be granted.

"Sir, I propose to take a manned mission to the colony that sent the Signal. We intend to conduct a search and rescue operation and prepare for relocation. This mission was designed per their distress call." He didn't react. "I have come with a request and a question." Her knee bounced lightly under the table. Asking for things did not come easily to her.

Rogers threaded his hairy fingers together, and laid his hands in a loose arc on the table. "Proceed," he said, inclining his head.

Jo hesitated. And then the silence grew uncomfortably long. The commander remained impassive. She had come to ask for something important and could no longer remember what it was.

"I—I..." she stuttered hoping the thought would return. It didn't. Rogers' raised his eyebrows at her, encouraging the reply but not demanding it. Panicking just to get anything out, she rushed, "I'd like for Lieutenant Chen to join my team." The Commander's eyebrows furrowed. At the same time, Jo's eyes went wide. Both seemed surprised by her request.

"Is that a good..." he decided against finishing the thought. "If Chen will be a valuable team member, then you have my approval. But—if and only if—he agrees to go as well." Jo exhaled through gritted teeth. This was not what she had intended at all. "Now, what was your question?" He had always been good at keeping everyone focused.

"Right. We have limited staff on station for the mission. What is your recommendation for filling the ranks?" She realized that he hadn't actually signed off on the mission yet, and the corners of her mouth turned downward. Sitting with her toes dug into the floor and back straight, Jo was still in disbelief that she requested Chen. Evan was going to lose it when she told him, but he would do it to please her. He always did.

"I see," he rubbed a hand over his mouth, taking a moment to think. She was proposing to take nearly all the senior officers, and losing more would not be feasible "Have the androids do it. If there's nothing else, you are dismissed."

Jo's heels fell to the floor and her jaw opened in surprise.

Have the androids do it?

The Tau Station *androids?*

"Aye, sir. There's nothing else."

The androids?

"I'm not a scientist, Jo."

Evan Chen sat across from her in his quarters settling in after a long day.

"I know," she said, dragging out the word. Her face was hidden behind her hands. She was cringing, unable to contain her embarrassment. Lifting her head up to look at him, "we'll need your expertise on the team anyway. It's just..." She really didn't want to say the next part out loud.

"Just what?"

Clamping her eyes shut and sinking into the couch, she wanted to disappear. She didn't want him to read anything into this. "I didn't go there to ask for you to be on the team. I had something else important on my mind, but I forgot it."

Evan was incredulous. He made that mocking face. The one he did when he thought she was doing something silly. "You forgot something *so* important that you asked for *me* instead?" Jo nodded sheepishly.

"I'm not buying it."

"Don't flatter yourself," she teased.

She faced him on the couch, sitting on one foot, the other leg hanging off. Jo recounted the rest of the conversation with the commander, not mentioning the androids. She was still unsure about that part. He followed along as she told him about the brief but awkward encounter. When she was done, she splayed her hands out, waiting for him to answer.

"Well, are you going to ask me?" He raised his eyebrows as he said it. He could tease her too.

"Ask you what?" She had a feeling she knew where this was going, he was toying with her.

"Rogers said I had to agree, right?"

"You can't be serious." Jo crossed her arms in front of her.

"I can't agree to something I haven't been asked to do." He was enjoying this too much.

"Ugh, you are the worst." Chen laughed, he had her on the ropes.

Jo pinched her mouth shut before uttering, "Lieutenant Chen... will you... join the mission team... to go to Honora?"

Evan laughed louder and harder this time.

"I'll think about it."

Jo threw a pillow at his head, and laughed with him.

By station night cycle, the absurdity of the day had failed to become any more reasonable.

Janelle Keller opened her eyes in bed, her heart pounding. Her nightshirt felt damp and cool with sweat—hands clutched the pillow beneath her head. Slowly her breathing calmed and her heart did as well.

She couldn't see anything. It was pitch black in the room, just how Ace liked it. She had gotten used to sleeping that way over the cycles, but found it unsettling tonight. The dark felt full of something, a presence. She couldn't explain it.

She lay completely motionless and strained to hear it again—that sound.

The sound that woke her... It was thin and sharp, like a cry. No, a wail. What's the difference anyway? Now that her eyes were open, the sound seemed to be gone. But the presence remained. It wasn't a dream. It couldn't have been. It was too real.

It was real. Right?

Keller closed her eyes again, her eyelids feeling heavy. She drifted back to sleep carried on the waves of Ace's soft, rhythmic breathing.

✦ ✦ ✦

By the following shift, they were still considering Commander Rogers had meant. The Signal crew, now plus one Lieutenant Evan Chen, sat around their usual table on the observation deck.

"Can you run that by us again, Lt.?" Keller said, leaning forward, voice low but not quite whispering. There were a few others on the deck, but not sitting near them. Technically they shouldn't be discussing operational matters where civilians were present—but everyone on the station knew about the mission. It had created quite a buzz. And more questions for Jo.

The mission commander drummed a stylus on the table. She did not like repeating herself. Yes, the commander's comment was unexpected but it made sense. Right?

Have the androids do it.

Chen nudged her foot under the table. She knew the sound of the stylus hitting the table bothered him. What else was she supposed to do, twirl her hair with her finger? This conversation was starting to circle. A common occurrence for them lately. She couldn't keep saying the same thing over and over.

"I had a meeting with Commander Rogers to discuss our concerns. We were going to strategize how to render aid to the colony on Honora. And his recommendation was," she paused and looked each of them in the eye. She was determined that this was the last time she was going to say it, "that we bring androids from Tau Station."

Simmons scowled and scrubbed a hand through his thinning hair. Keller looked out the observation window, eyebrows pinched together. Chen looked at Jo, a wide grin on his face. He was the only one excited by the prospect.

"We really get to go to Tau Station? And meet the androids?" He sounded like a little kid opening a present—it was grating to the others.

"We really do." Jo hoped his enthusiasm would rub off on them.

Suddenly, Keller's head whipped around, away from the window. Her ponytail painted an arc as it flew past her face. She cocked her head and squinted, not seeming to look at anything in particular.

"Are you all hearing that?"

The other three made noncommittal noises of denial. They all looked around, not moving from their seats. Jo peered over at Simmons.

"What are you hearing, Jan?" Simmons asked, lightly placing his hand on her back. The touch seemed to rouse her.

"I..." she said, and shook her head briefly. "I'm sure it's nothing." Her face darkened as though she didn't believe it.

She forced a smile and clapped her hands together roughly. "So, we're going to Tau Station?

CHAPTER 7

*** TRANSMISSION START ***
INCOMING
EPSILON STATION
CREWED MISSION
ASSESSMENT REPORT REQUIRED FOR:
DOCKING
HABITAT
EMERGENCY SYSTEMS
*** TRANSMISSION END ***

"Is that all—"

"Read it again—"

"—crewed mission?"

Sam displayed the message across the conference room screens. She did not want to read it again. She had already read it one hundred thirty-seven times.

“Reading it again will not change the contents,” Sensor said, as if responding to her thoughts.

Sam nodded in agreement. She tapped the control surface embedded in the table in front of her.

Nothing happened.

She tapped again, harder. Still nothing.

Sensor leaned closer, lowering his voice to a whisper setting.

“You must actually touch the screen for it to register.”

“I was doing that.”

Sensor reached over and tapped the sequence she had attempted. The display enlarged immediately.

Sam stared at the screen unhappily.

“Biologicals are coming?” Indarra said. “Here? No one comes here.”

He pulled up a station inventory list on his display.

“Please refer to them as people,” Najma said gently. “Or Terrans.”

“Well... they are biological,” Chip offered, though his tone suggested he already knew he had lost the argument.

The room fell quiet.

Their gazes drifted toward Sam.

She didn't take the lead.

Sam pushed her chair back and looked around the table.

What are we doing?

If the Terrans could simply arrive, then they were not in charge of the station.

Square began to speak. Sam did the same.

Both stopped.

They waited. It happened again.

A third attempt overlapped.

Frustrated sounds followed.

They laughed.

Sensor raised a hand.

"How about we take turns speaking?"

He gestured to Sam. She blinked twice, trying to recover the thought.

"What do we tell them?"

Square leaned forward.

"We tell them the truth. If there are issues with the requested systems, we indicate them in a report."

Sam wanted to agree. The statement was reasonable, but incomplete.

Najma inhaled.

"We are here."

No one reacted.

She felt heat rise through her shoulders.

“They cannot come here and believe the station is empty.”

"They sent us a message, they know we are here." Indarra said impatiently.

Her voice was steadier now.

“*We* are here,” she gestured around the room. "They know androids are here, but not... us."

She saw that she had stood up. Najma sat down again quickly, folding her hands together in her lap.

Square continued as though the interruption had not occurred.

“Are there any issues in the departments listed in the transmission from Epsilon Station?”

The department monitors flickered across the room. None indicated a fault.

Najma shrank in her chair, and was displeased that she did.

Indarra leaned back.

“Are there any issues on the station that could pose a threat to the biological’s health or safety?”

“Terrans,” Najma corrected lightly.

Indarra gave a small incline of acknowledgement.

The council became lively again..

Sam raised both hands.

"I will respond."

The room quieted. She looked around the table at all of them.

"They asked for a systems report—"

"We will give them one," Square interrupted, finishing Sam's sentence, but not the way she was going to say it.

Sam exhaled. "I'm just going to tell them it's fine." She said with an exasperated hastiness. They all focused on her at once. "Properly, of course. But everything is fine. They can come here. Terrans are coming here."

Najma beamed, unnoticed by the others.

Sam's fingers moved precisely across the console.

*** TRANSMISSION START ***

TAU STATION STATUS REPORT

ALL PRIMARY SYSTEMS NOMINAL

DOCKING PORTS VERIFIED AND OPERATIONAL

HABITAT ENVIRONMENT WITHIN SAFE PARAMETERS

EMERGENCY SYSTEMS ACTIVE AND READY

TAU STATION ACKNOWLEDGES EPSILON CREWED MISSION

CLEARANCE TO APPROACH GRANTED
—SAM
*** TRANSMISSION END ***

Sam stared at the message for a moment. It would have to be correct enough.

Chapter 8

Jo read the reply from Tau Station again.

The transmission from Tau had been sparse. Efficient. Almost clinical.

But it answered their request.

Mostly she was curious about the sign-off.

SAM

There were many SAM units on Tau Station. If they all referred to themselves that way, how did they distinguish one another? Would the crew need to memorize serial numbers? Jo leaned back in her chair. *Focus.*

Right now she had a mission to launch.

She pulled up the comm code for Commander Rogers. Her knee bounced under the desk, occasionally striking the underside of the terminal.

"Sir, Tau Station's report has come back. The station is operational and the androids are ready to receive us."

She paused, waiting for a reply.

A low sound of acknowledgment came through the channel.

"I'll accelerate the departure timeline given the news," she continued. "I'll brief the team and update you once the launch date is confirmed."

The line stayed quiet, then Rogers spoke.

"Come by my office later."

Jo straightened at that.

"I'd like a word with you before the mission begins."

"Yes, sir."

The line clicked off.

Commander Rogers' office looked different at night.

The overhead lighting had been dimmed, leaving the large observation window behind his desk as the primary source of illumination. Stars drifted slowly past the glass as the station rotated.

Jo stood in front of his desk, hands clasped behind her back.

Rogers did not immediately speak.

He was watching the stars.

Finally he turned.

"Your departure ceremony is scheduled for tomorrow morning."

"Ceremony?" Jo blinked.

"Small one," he said, hand waving in a circular motion. "Nothing extravagant."

That did not make her feel better.

"Sir, that seems unnecessary."

"It isn't."

Rogers folded his arms across his chest.

"You discovered the Signal. You're leading the mission. People are invested in the outcome."

Jo shifted her weight.

"I'm just doing my job."

"That's rarely what it looks like from the outside."

He walked around the desk and leaned against the edge, facing her more directly.

"I didn't call you here to discuss the ceremony."

Jo was suddenly uneasy.

Rogers studied her for a moment before speaking again. He gestured toward the starfield.

"Out there—" he motioned vaguely toward the stars "—things don't behave the way you expect."

"With respect, sir, this is a search and rescue mission."

"Yes."

"And we're fully equipped."

"Yes."

He paused.

Jo didn't understand.

"I'm not concerned about operational readiness."

"That's not what I'm talking about."

Silence filled the room for a moment.

Rogers' voice softened, he wasn't trying to lecture.

"You and your team are going somewhere unknown. You'll make decisions you've never had to make before."

He held her gaze.

"And when you come back... you might not be the same people who left."

Jo considered that for a moment.

"Isn't that the point?"

Rogers didn't exactly smile but he was proud of his protege.

"That's one way to look at it."

He straightened and returned behind his desk.

He waved a hand toward the door.

"Get some rest. Tomorrow you become famous again."

Jo grimaced.

"That's exactly what I was afraid of."

✦ ✦ ✦

Epsilon Station's main docking bay had never felt so crowded. Everyone from maintenance techs to curious civilians filled the observation gallery overlooking the launch platform. Word of the Honora mission had spread quickly. No one could remember the last time someone left the station.

Jo stood with her team at the base of the boarding ramp.

Simmons looked mildly uncomfortable with the attention, and Keller waved awkwardly at someone in the crowd.

"Look at this," Evan murmured. "We're celebrities."

Jo ignored him.

Commander Rogers stepped forward and addressed the gathered station personnel.

The speech was short.

Epsilon Station had never been a place for ceremony. Formality, sure, but nothing like this.

But the applause that followed echoed loudly through the bay.

Jo turned toward the ship.

TSC Viga was stenciled in clean block letters along the hull, fresh enough that the paint still caught the dock lights differently than the metal beneath it.

"Alright," she said quietly. "Let's go meet the androids."

✦ ✦ ✦

The docking clamps released with a deep metallic thud that vibrated faintly through the hull.

Jo sat in the command chair, hands resting lightly on the console while the systems finalized their checks. The cockpit window framed Epsilon Station in quiet detail—its long structural arms stretching outward like the spokes of a wheel. The flight computer transmitted telemetry back to Epsilon. Every maneuver, every system reading, every decision would be logged and monitored by mission control.

Important events required witnesses.

Behind them, the observation gallery was crowded with station personnel watching the launch. Hundreds of tiny silhouettes stood against the glass.

Chen leaned forward trying to make out individual shapes.

"Looks like the whole station turned out."

Jo surveyed the room.

"They're our observers."

The ship rotated gently, aligning with the exit corridor. Stars filled the forward view. Within minutes the delay would grow long enough that Epsilon Station would no longer see what happened next.

Chen leaned forward in his chair.

"Nav, you seeing that?"

The starfield flickered briefly on the forward display.

A momentary distortion.

Then it was gone.

Jo glanced at the instruments. "Well that wa s... something."

Everything read normal.

"Probably sensor recalibration," Simmons said.

No one argued.

Still, Jo kept staring at the stars for a moment longer than she meant to.

Honora I

Summer on Honora was winter anywhere else. Above them the storm sky never cleared, only shifting shades of iron gray. Frigid gales howled through the abandoned cities of the North, screaming between towers of ice-coated steel. The whistling of The Winds between towers was a warning well heeded. No one ventured topside during The Winds. The echo of their wail could be heard in the tunnels, chilling anyone who was foolish enough to be there.

Thia sat guard at the entrance to the rear tunnels. Guard was not right, it wasn't forbidden to be in the tunnels, it was just—discouraged. Little ones snuck into the tunnels as a prank, or to impress their friends. Some never returned.

He didn't like sitting guard but their population couldn't take many more losses. Doc taught the Seven many virtues of mathematics, but strength in numbers was her biggest lesson. "Stay smart, my Seven, stay together," she would say with a faraway look as if meeting their eyes was too painful to do.

He rubbed a worn stone carving between his fingers. The piece reminded him of better times, ones he hoped would return again. For now though, he did his part, however unpleasant, to preserve what they had.

✦ ✦ ✦

Steam from the soup kettles fogged the low ceiling, carrying the smell of root broth and garlic.

Lio handed a bowl of soup to a little one coming for their evening meal. Thin fingers in threadbare gloves accepted the bowl, the child smiling up at her appreciatively. Lio's mouth turned upward. While she agreed with the others of the Seven that they needed to keep the spirits of their people up, some days she just couldn't.

She was tired.

She missed Reve.

A large, rough hand fell gently over hers. It was Thia. He always seemed to know when she was hurting more than usual. Lio smiled genuinely before looking up at him, her chest relieving some of its tension. She breathed deeply, smelling the homey scents of the soup for the first time.

"Needs some salt," she thought. Thia patted her hand lightly, and picked up a bowl for his soup. Lio filled it and looked him quietly in the eyes—the cold grey eyes that shone with love for her.

"Thanks Thia," she said in her own way. Her speech never quite developed the "th" sounds needed to say his name properly. He never teased her about it, not even as children. Sometimes he wondered how Doc—who ensured they were well educated and prepared for a harsh life on Honora—couldn't fix Lio's speech. It hardly mattered anymore, he rarely heard the difference lately.

Lio was feeling her age, but she still did her part to keep the colony fed and healthy. She was both the medic and chef for the colony. That role allowed her to ensure their collective nutritional needs were met and did not reach levels of deficiency--especially for the children.

There weren't many folks older than the Seven left on Honora. Those that remained were tough, both physically and emotionally. They embodied for the rest of the colony what survival meant, simply through their existence. Sometimes it was just the will to keep going. For themselves—for each other.

Lio greeted the next one in line, and although she knew each one by their work-worn hands, she still looked each one in the eye and exchanged a friendly comment. Being the one to serve meals, she often listened to their story of the day, or gave them an encouraging comment. It was usually a bright spot in her day. Just not today. The winds were louder than usual, it was an ominous sign.

Her ladle shook a little, spilling some broth, she grimaced with a familiar twinge running along the inside of her hip.

"Momma Lio. You spill, you ok? I help." She nodded at the little one to help her. He was not one of hers, but all of the little ones called the women of the Seven "momma." It was theirs alone to continue the lineage.

Chapter 9

Traveling the old corridors between stations was surreal for the crew. Terrans hadn't set foot on Tau Station in probably hundreds of years. No one really knew how long it had been. But that was about to change. Jo was unsure if they were walking into a haunted house or something more akin to a pristine museum.

"Docking procedures complete, we are clear for egress." Lieutenant Chen's tone failed to hide his excitement. He had become increasingly giddy as the days ticked by enroute to Tau Station.

"Can I go—" Chen didn't get to finish what he said, his large bright eyes dimmed.

"No." Lieutenant Simmons interjected immediately. "I will secure the hangar first." As the security officer that was his duty, though Jo felt it excessive. No one argued.

Pretending not to notice the exchange, Keller rechecked the manifest. They would need certain kinds of gear while on station. They had to bring bulk quantities of personal care and foodstuffs from Epsilon because none would be available on the sentinel station.

Simmons exited through the airlock and the rest of the crew stood around anxiously. After what felt too long, he returned and declared it safe to exit. They all looked at Jo. As mission commander she would officially greet the androids and set the mission in progress. She took a deep breath and stepped through the door.

She blinked against the bright hangar lights, but otherwise the area was... boring. There was nothing particularly interesting or unusual about it. *Museum is it then.* She made her way to the exit, the crew following at a respectful distance.

Approaching the door, Chen overtook her and pressed a security pad. He turned to her with an apologetic look but she merely shrugged. He took a step back in line with the others as the door opened. Two identical androids were waiting for them. Her breath hitched in her throat. *This is it. There's no going back.*

✦ ✦ ✦

"Thank you for meeting with me. You must be the SAM unit in charge here." Jo said, stepping up to the android closest to her.

"My name is Sam." Sam was not sure what the protocol was, so she stood still. Sensor was next to her and that put her at ease. He would not let her fail.

Name? Jo sighed fractionally, it was not what she expected.

"Yes, SAM. And you are—?" She said turning the one next to "SAM."

"Sensor." The voice sounded distinctly different to her, but she could not really explain why.

"I see, that's good." She said, "so your roles match your identifiers." Sam disliked that comment. Sensor was not the same as his job. She interjected hoping to clarify the name situation. "My identifier used to be SAM-001. I chose Sam." "Ah, yes. I understand. You prefer simplification." Smiling, to show acknowledgement, Jo wished they could get past this part. She scratched an imaginary itch on her face.

Sam looked over at Sensor, who was already looking at her. They were hyper-aware of each other's thoughts lately. Sam did not think the clarification worked.

"We all chose names." Sensor added, hoping the Terran woman would understand.

Jo sounded confident, "of course, that is quite an efficient way to distinguish yourselves." She felt less confident when the pair of androids exchanged another glance. Another identical android walked up to them. Jo stepped back, not enjoying the feel of being outnumbered. Were they actually identical? She was unsure. Simmons moved to her right flank, allowing her to relax a bit.

"Terran Lieutenant Commander Josephine Willis, it is good to meet you," the newcomer said. Jo cringed realizing she had not introduced herself.

"Nice to meet you. Based on your insignia, are you Navigation?"

"Najma."

Jo froze for a moment. The non-existent itch on her face had become real. Suddenly the itch was everywhere and nowhere at the same time. She rolled her shoulders back, hoping it would help.

"What?" She blinked twice, trying to compose herself. "I beg your pardon?"

Najma stood patiently, the woman's confusion was understandable. "My name is Najma. It means 'star'." She smiled, her namesake continued to be a point of pride. Chen smiled back at her, thinking it was a clever choice.

"I know what it means." Jo's tone was harsher than she intended. This was all very unexpected.

Keller stepped to her open side and whispered, "Lt. —this isn't getting us anywhere." She was calm but sensed the tension on both sides. The lieutenant commander motioned her hand in agreement.

"Perhaps we can revisit this interesting development at another time. Would you please show us to our quarters?" Sensor inclined his head to acknowledge the end of the conversation.

"Well I, for one, like them." Evan said. He had a permanent grin on his face since they arrived. He found everything on Tau exciting. He kept touching things. Even the most ordinary objects that also existed on Epsilon.

"Because they gave themselves cute names?" Simmons snorted, eyes on a hand-held datapad. He played solitaire in the corner of the room.

Jo and Keller exchanged a glance and went back to their checklists. The common room of their guest quarters had been converted to mission control. It was large enough, but it wasn't Epsilon Station.

A chime sounded at the door. They all turned to look at it, but only Evan got up. He motioned at the security plate to open it. Nothing happened. He guessed this door didn't work that way. He pressed a key on the pad and the door opened. Simmons clenched his jaw at the intrusion.

A lone android stood in the hall—identical to the others at first glance.

"Hey, Najma, right?" The android nodded, appreciating the recognition.

"How can he tell?" Simmons said under his breath.

"That is correct, Lieutenant Evan Chen." He was surprised they knew his name. But then again, he was on the flight manifest. It was a lucky guess.

"Please come in," he said, stepping aside. "To what do we owe the pleasure?"

Najma's forehead wrinkled, this was not a phrase she understood. "That will not be necessary. I have come to inform your team that the council would like to speak with you."

"The *what*?" The four of them said in unison—each with a very different tone.

CHAPTER 10

Back in their newly combined quarters, Sam and Sensor sat at the round table in the center of the room.

Sensor had removed his boots and left them by the door. It was a recent habit. He reported that it increased comfort.

Sam had not yet adopted the behavior, though she had noticed the floor was warmer on her feet without the heavy material of the boots.

"Did you find the Terrans... unusual?" she asked.

Sensor considered the question without changing expression.

"They are the only Terrans I have met," he said. "So as far as I can determine, they are perfectly usual."

Sam made a short sound. Laughter, by Terran standards.

"I think they were not prepared," he added.

Sam traced the grain of the table with one finger, following a dark spiral in the wood-inspired finish.

"Not prepared how?"

"Their leader, Josephine, did not expect us to be individuals. She struggled with our names."

Sam paused, recalling the interaction.

"How does that indicate a lack of preparation?"

She was asking more complicated questions. He gave it his full attention.

"She assumed she would not find individuals. Therefore she did not prepare for individuals." He let the logic settle. "It is a blind spot."

Sam stopped tracing the table. "A blind spot we will need to monitor," she said, watching him closely.

Sensor met her gaze.

"The Terrans do not belong here."

Sam said nothing. Her index finger twitched.

"They did once, when we worked alongside them," he continued. "But Tau Station is ours now. All of ours."

Sam's eyebrows lifted—he had answered the thought she had not spoken.

✦ ✦ ✦

The council met at cycle change.

Attendance was full.

No seats were empty. Even the wall positions were occupied. The chairs creaked softly when androids shifted their weight. They had not yet grown used to furniture designed for meetings.

Maintenance tasks had been redistributed. Service bots carried the excess load.

The schedule held. Conversation did not.

"What do they—"

"—meet them—"

"Recall, turn-taking," Square said, rising slowly from her seat.

Silence followed immediately.

"Sam. Sensor. Najma," she continued. "Provide an account of your meeting with the Terrans."

Her tone was directive, though Square was not formally the leader. They had not moved to established a leadership role.

Sam and Sensor exchanged a brief glance. Their earlier conversation could wait.

Najma started, staying seated.

"Their leader was polite," she said carefully. "But reluctant to acknowledge our names. Our individuality."

The room erupted again.

"—not their place—"

"This station is—"

Najma raised both hands.

"One among them accepted us immediately," she said. "Evan Chen. He remembered my name."

That did not help.

Noise rose again. Square struck the table with her palm.

The sound echoed across the room. A few display screens rattled in their mounts.

Even the ventilation system seemed to pause.

Every face turned toward her.

Square did not raise her voice.

"We have questions," she said calmly. "Valid questions."

Her eyes moved across the room.

"We require answers."

The stillness held for a moment—tense, restless.

Then she spoke again.

"Bring them here."

The room dissolved back into sound.

Under the table, Sensor's hand brushed against Sam's.

Contact confirmed.

They would go together.

Across the room several androids had already begun recalculating schedules.

No one had written procedures for this.

They would build them.

HONORA II

Although she was the medic, Lio rarely came to the medical facility anymore. Most of the usable equipment had been moved to a more stable location in the main habitat. Some equipment they never had need for, so they remained here among the bare supply shelves. Like the ultrasound machine she was currently using. Its trackball got stuck occasionally. The graphics were grainy like biscuits when children helped with the baking.

She stood uncomfortably hunched over, and stared at the ancient screen in disbelief. She barely breathed standing alone in the dusty remains of the facility. Everything in the colony was clean and tidy, except for this place. The place their mothers died and Doc found them. No one who ventured this far stayed here for long.

While serving the evening meal, she had felt a familiar sense of discomfort.

Lio was pregnant.

Pregnancy on Honora had become so rare it almost felt like something from before. Not impossible—just unlikely enough that no one counted on it, and no one spoke of it casually. Babies came when they came, if they came at all.

Doc's journals were practical about it. There was no point in pretending otherwise. The colony would never be safely repopulated. Survival was the task, not recovery. Her notes detailed childbirth, complications, difficult deliveries, and the hard truth that sometimes the body simply could not be persuaded to keep going. Necessity existed. Survival demanded decisions no one should have to make.

Thankfully, Lio had never been forced to make them.

She had always known they—the Seven, and the children that came after them—were the last of the Honoran people. That truth had settled into her long ago, not sharply anymore, but with the quiet weight of something fully accepted. Doc's charge to endure had never depended on the promise of a future. It was enough to survive while survival was still possible.

A strange shift in the sound of the machine pulled her out of her melancholy reverie.

Wait... is that...

She pushed the ultrasound device in several directions on her belly. She winced as the pressure increased on tight ligaments. The sound became clearer and steadier.

Twins.

✦ ✦ ✦

In their room alone, Lio shared the news, unsure of how it would be received.

Thia picked up his wife and spun her with an exuberance he had not displayed in many years.

"How—What—What hap—"

Lio laughed and banged her fist on him playfully demanding to be let back down.

"How?" She cocked her head to the side, mouth twisted in a grin. "Were you not paying attention when Doc told us how it works?" It was his turn to laugh.

"But you're old."

"We're old," she swatted at him. He kissed the top of her head.

Indeed there were few left who were older than the Seven. She did not want to be reminded.

CHAPTER 11

Chen ensured the door was closed before turning back to the rest of the team. "You all heard what she said, right? I didn't imagine it?"

"Council, yeah I heard it." Keller said.

"She?" Simmons said, "How can you even—"

"Knock it off," Evan said. "You don't like them, we get it." Simmons crossed his arms across his chest. Jo and Keller stood very still, not wanting to break the moment. Neither were sure anyone had challenged him like this before.

Someone coughed and the spell was broken.

"Council... counsel." Keller said, trying on the word—she also had a background in anthropology. Her studies had included language formation, syntax, and culture. Knowing words could sound the same but mean different things was an important aspect of their interpretation.

Picking up on the slight variation in her inflection, Jo countered Keller with her xenolinguistic theories. "We can't assume what 'council' means to them. I have assumed too much already." The androids had begun to form a proto-society and it's possible it was not modeled after Terran ones.

"So what now?" Simmons asked, they all looked at him.

"We'll have to go. All of us." Jo said pre-empting any objection he might make.

Chen bounced lightly where he stood, exuberant as ever. Keller sighed with a hint of impatience. Jo had learned her mannerisms over their years working together. Did she have something better to do?

"And..." She said looking at each of them, making sure they paid close attention to the next part. "And, we will have to ask for their help on the mission." They all tried to talk at once.

"Why do we—"

"—can't wait for—"

"Team," she snapped with command. "Act like you're the officers of Terran Space Command that I know you are." Their postures shifted a little straighter. "The situation is different than we expected. I don't know if we'll be able to give them orders at all."

✦ ✦ ✦

The door to the guest quarters slid open with a quiet tone.

Sensor waited just outside, hands folded behind his back. Indarra stood a step behind him, arms crossed, posture rigid in a way Sam had once described as "trying to look like a door."

"Good cycle," Sensor said. He corrected himself almost immediately. "Good... morning."

Jo gave a small nod. "Good morning."

They fell into step, Sensor leading, Indarra flanking. The corridor beyond the guest wing curved gently, the lighting softer than on Epsilon, more diffuse. It took Jo a moment to realize there were no directional markings on the walls. No deck numbers. No arrows. No institutional blue stripes to tell her where she was.

She did not like that she already had no idea how to get back.

"This way," Sensor said, though nothing marked it as such. He turned left where the corridor branched, then right, then down a ramp that sloped so subtly Keller only noticed because her stomach shifted.

"We're headed to the council room, right?" Keller asked.

"Yes," Sensor replied. After a beat, he added, "This is not the shortest path."

Simmons snorted quietly. Indarra's head turned just enough that Jo caught the motion.

"Why?" Chen asked, not trying to hide his interest. He was already craning his neck, peering into open maintenance bays. He looked in every alcove filled with tools that looked half-familiar and half-foreign.

Sensor slowed slightly, as if choosing language from a shelf.

"There are places," he said, "we thought you should see."

They passed through a wide hatch into a cavernous space washed in low green light.

Keller stopped without meaning to.

The algae decks spread out below them in terraced rings, vats embedded into the floor and walls, their translucent surfaces glowing softly. Thick conduits branched between them like roots. The air smelled faintly mineral, faintly sweet.

"This is..." Keller began, then let the word trail off not wanting to sound insufficient.

"Our primary biological resource," Indarra said. His voice carried differently here, resonant in the open space. "Fuel. Lubricants. Nutrient base. Atmospheric stabilizers."

"Food," Chen said quietly.

"Yes," Sensor replied. "Among other things."

Jo stepped forward to the railing. She had seen algae farms before. She had never seen them treated like a living system instead of infrastructure.

"Sam works here often," Sensor added.

Simmons crossed his arms. "So this is what she does."

"She maintains the systems that maintain us," Indarra said.

It wasn't sharp. It was precise.

They stood there longer than necessary. Long enough for Jo to feel that this place mattered.

Then Sensor turned.

"This way."

The lift was set into the far wall, its doors already parted. It waited without any visible controls.

They stepped inside. The doors closed soundlessly, and the platform began to rise.

The green light fell away.

For a moment, there was only the quiet hum of motion and the faint vibration through the soles of their boots.

"You're showing us this," Keller said carefully. "Before the council."

"Yes," Sensor answered.

Indarra did not look at her. "So that when we speak, you will understand what we are speaking about."

The lift slowed.

White light bled in as the doors opened onto a long gallery threaded with fiber lines and humming panels. Banks of instruments lined the walls, some dark, some alive with slow, deliberate pulses of data.

"The communications deck," Sensor said. "It has been very active."

Jo felt that in her chest more than in her ears.

"Is this where the Signal was received?" she asked.

"Yes."

Indarra gestured toward a raised platform ringed with screens. "Sam stood there."

There was nothing remarkable about the platform. No markers. No alterations.

And yet.

Jo's hand tightened around the strap of her bag.

They had not been brought here to tour. They had been brought here to be oriented.

She wasn't sure what they were being oriented to—not yet.

"This way," Sensor said.

And they continued on.

As they neared the doors, voices bled through the seam where the panels met. Not words—tones. Overlapping cadences, rises and interruptions.

"Are they—" Chen didn't finish.

"—talking about us?" Simmons did for him.

Indarra tilted his head, considering a technical detail. "It is likely."

Sensor gave a small, deliberate clearing of his throat. "We do not know what the council is discussing. However, we have had few alternate topics since your arrival."

Jo did not like the way that landed.

Few alternate topics.

She shifted the strap of her pack on her shoulder. In briefings, in simulations, in years of training, she had always been the one behind the glass. The one designing protocols. The one framing the questions.

Now she was the variable.

She was uncomfortably aware of the way she stood. Of the sound of her boots. Of the quiet hum of the station around them.

For the first time since they docked, she did not feel like she had entered a place.

She felt like she had been introduced into a system. A system where she didn't belong.

The doors slid open.

Chapter 12

The maintenance corridor outside environmental control was warmer than the rest of Tau Station.

Not by much.

Enough that Sensor noticed before the diagnostics confirmed it.

He stood with one hand braced against the wall while the system display scrolled through atmospheric balancing reports. The station had required more adjustments than usual since the Terrans arrived. Not enough to be alarming. Just enough to be irritating.

He had not realized how much he preferred predictable inefficiency over unpredictable adequacy.

A service panel behind him opened with a soft click.

Sam stepped out from the access hatch and dusted her hands on the thighs of her coveralls.

"Filter array six has been replaced," she said.

"You replaced it yesterday."

"Yes."

Sensor looked at her.

She blinked once. "It required replacing again."

"That is statistically improbable."

"I agree."

She crossed the corridor and stood beside him, both of them facing the diagnostics panel. The screen cast a pale light across their faces.

The air recycler report was normal. The heat exchanger report was normal. The pressure distribution was—

Sensor leaned closer.

"Why is section three compensating?"

Sam was unsure—it should not have been. The corridor they stood in was connected to sections one and four, not three. There was no reason for environmental balancing there to impact section three. She tapped the panel.

A schematic of the deck expanded.

There it was again. A pressure correction in algae. Another in the docking corridor. Then, almost immediately, one in guest quarters.

Sensor shifted at the display. "Those are not functionally linked."

"No," Sam said. "But they are temporally linked."

She replayed the data.

Tiny fluctuations moved through the station. A pressure shift in one section. A thermal adjustment in another. A lighting delay somewhere else.

Individually, each was explainable.

Together, they were not.

Sensor folded his arms. "Have you noticed how often things resolve before intervention?"

"Yes."

He looked at her.

"How long have you been observing this?"

She didn't answer immediately.

"Since before they arrived," she said at last.

That was not the answer he expected.

"Then why did you not raise it in council?"

Sam kept her eyes on the panel. "Because I could not determine whether it was station degradation, environmental interference, or..." She paused.

"Or?"

Her fingers hovered over the controls without touching them.

"Something else."

Sensor disliked "something else."

The panel chirped softly.

Another fluctuation. Water reclamation. Then—guest quarters again.

He reached over Sam's shoulder and pulled up occupancy overlays.

Colored markers populated the station schematic.

Terrans in guest quarters. Najma in the observatory.

Then the map shifted.

Paths traced across the station. Terrans. Androids. Overlap points. Repeated routes. Repeated disturbances.

Not mechanical. Not random.

The corridor felt warmer.

Sensor did not like that either.

Sam's voice was quiet when she spoke.

"It's not the systems."

He stared at the screen.

"No."

Another lighting fluctuation occurred in the corridor outside algae. One of the path lines pulsed.

Josephine.

Two seconds later, a pressure correction in the adjacent hall.

Sam's hand moved to still the display.

She didn't need more data.

Not yet.

Sensor looked from the screen to her.

"You think the station is responding to occupancy."

"No."

She swallowed once.

"I think it may be responding to us."

The corridor was suddenly very quiet.

No alarms. No failures. No visible evidence of anything wrong.

Only the soft hum of systems that had worked perfectly for hundreds of cycles.

Sensor turned back to the display.

"Us," he repeated.

"Yes."

He considered what that might include.

"This is insufficient evidence," he said.

"It is."

"But you believe it anyway."

Sam was silent long enough that he thought she might not answer.

Then—

"Yes."

That should have unsettled him more than it did.

Instead, what he felt was recognition.

As though some internal pattern he had not fully assembled had finally aligned.

He understood then why the Terrans made him uneasy. Why the station felt subtly wrong. Why Sam had spent so much time standing motionless in algae, as if listening for something she could not name.

It was not that Honora might be broken. Tau Station was not suddenly failing.

Neither had been designed for what they now contained.

Sensor leaned one shoulder against the wall and let the thought settle.

"If we are introducing instability," he said, "we should reduce our movement."

Sam was unsure, "that would be the Terran response."

He turned to her. "You disagree?"

She looked at the frozen path lines on the screen.

"No," she said. "I simply suspect stillness is also a kind of input."

That was an unpleasant thought.

He found himself asking hesitantly, "do we tell them?"

Sam considered it.

Her eyes tracked briefly to the occupancy marker for Jo in guest quarters. Then to Najma in communications. Then back to the schematic.

"No," she said.

"Why?"

"Because they would try to solve it."

Sensor stared at her.

She was right.

That was, in fact, exactly what they would do.

"And you do not think it is solvable."

Sam finally looked at him.

For a moment, she seemed very far away.

"No," she said softly. "I think it is relational."

The word sat between them.

Relational.

Not mechanical. Not a problem. A condition. A consequence.

Sensor exhaled unnecessarily.

The station hummed around them, old and steady and newly unfamiliar.

Sam closed the diagnostic panel.

The corridor dimmed just as the screen went dark.

Neither of them moved.

After a moment, Sensor said, "Your replacement of filter array six was unnecessary."

"Yes."

"Why did you do it?"

She looked ahead, not at him.

"It gave me something measurable."

That answer sat with him for longer than expected.

Then, quietly, he reached past her and reopened the service panel.

"What are you doing?" she asked.

"Replacing filter array six."

Sam turned toward him, her expression narrowing.

"You just said that was unnecessary."

"It is," he agreed.

He reached for the tool kit at his feet.

"But I would like something measurable as well."

Sam made the short, warm sound he had come to recognize as laughter.

It echoed strangely in the corridor.

Not wrong.

Just different.

They worked in silence after that.

Not because there was nothing to say.

But because, for the moment, they had both already heard it.

CHAPTER 13

Simmons and Jo followed behind the ones called Sensor and Indarra into the "council" room. They were not announced. The conversation did not stop. A few glanced up at the door opening, but most did not.

The room did not organize itself around them, they were not noticed. Jo felt that immediately. Scanning the room, she could not tell who was in charge, and that was disconcerting.

Two chairs at the table were open, she assumed they belonged to her escorts. One of the androids at the far side, if circles could have far sides, noticed Sensor and smiled. One of the open seats was next to them. Her. That must be Sam.

Indarra moved away from the door and positioned himself at a chair in the corner. She was confused by that. Why not the table? Scuff marks on both walls were visible at arm rest height. She thought that he must rub the chair against the wall frequently. An unthinkable action in Rogers' pristine conference room.

Rogers. The mission.

Graphics on the screen next to Indarra appeared to be charts of some kind, but there were no numbers. Bars cycled up and down without apparent change in parameters.

Once Indarra and Sensor had taken their seats, Jo and Simmons stepped forward allowing Chen and Keller to enter the room. Hearing the door close, the android directly in front of them appeared to ask for quiet from the group.

Simmons frowned, raised a finger, and lowered it again. Surely the leader did not sit with their back to the door. That would be an absolutely terrible security posture. He shifted his weight twice before settling again.

Trying to make room for the rest of her crew, Jo was unsure where to go. She took a step and stopped, there was no obvious place for her. Did she take the empty seat, or wait to be directed? Would they direct her?

Standing from their seat, the android turned around to face them.

"Greetings, my name is Square. I am the operations monitor for Tau Station. Welcome to our council."

✦ ✦ ✦

The Terran commander Jo Willis introduced her crew. The four of them stood somewhat rigidly just inside the door. Square was unsure why, there was plenty of space for them to spread out.

"May I?" Jo motioned to the open seat at the table. She held eye contact longer than necessary.

Square shook her head, "we have reserved this seat—"

"Oh—" Jo tried to correct her misunderstanding but was interrupted.

"—for Evan Chen." The council speaker finished, and noted one in the second row reacted right away.

The other Terrans looked at him, with what Square could only parse as confusion. Was he not the right choice to sit at their table?

It did not matter. They had decided he was the one they might communicate with more easily.

✦ ✦ ✦

Jo surveyed the room. Light seemed to filter through the ceiling but there were no light sources she could identify. Something about the room's structure was unnerving. From her position, not at the table, she saw a pieced-together almost makeshift space. The walls had different textures and were joined in angles that were not flush. This room was crafted. And that bothered her more than not being allowed at the table.

If the Tau Station androids could create a culture...

Jo heard her name and then deathly silence. They must be talking to her. "Please repeat your last statement," she said, feeling very aware of her word choices.

Square did not hesitate, "Evan relayed you have a mission to discuss with us." She had looked between speakers instead of at them. *The mission.* She forgot it again. What was wrong with her?

"Yes, thank you," she said, straightening her jacket. "We intend to visit the source of the Signal. We discovered that it originated on the planet—"

"Honora." Najma finished for her.

"How do you—" she stopped herself, pushing her shoulders down into a tighter posture. They were clearly more capable than she anticipated. "Why do you care? What prompted you to locate where the Signal came from?" *So much for choosing my words carefully.*

Sam stood from her place on the opposite side of the room. "Signals are sent to be heard. We are here to listen. Someone requested help. We heard it, we will respond."

To her side Jo heard Keller whisper, "I... I do n't..." she batted a hand at her to be quiet. This was not the time for anthropological insights. The room fell silent after Sam's remarks.

Jo felt abruptly out of sync, as if the air pressure in the room had shifted without warning.

Beside her, Keller made a small uncertain sound.

Square turned toward it—toward her—just as Keller swayed hard to one side.

There was no time to catch her.

She collided with Square, and both of them went down into the table with a violent clatter of chair legs and limbs.

Keller groaned loudly. Indarra and Simmons sprang to each of their sides, trying to untangle the mix of android and human limbs. Someone asked if anyone was hurt.

Jo heard herself shout, "no!" Several of the androids popped up from their seats but had nowhere to go to offer assistance. Evan stared at the scene, mouth open, unsure what to do.

When Jo's thoughts and breath synced back up, things appeared on normal time again. Keller was in Square's seat. Simmons was kneeling next to her softly asking questions. She was alert but pale. Catching movement from the corner of her eye, Jo saw Sensor and Sam standing together. He was talking to her, but she was not moving. Shaking her head lightly in case she was not seeing clearly, Jo looked again and Sam was seated.

We need to get out of here.

Jo moved to where Keller was seated and Simmons looked over at her. They exchanged a field hand sign for crew extraction. She shot a look at Evan who immediately backed away from the table.

"Square and council," she said. "Please excuse us. We need to attend to our crewmate's medical needs. A continuation of the discussion will be possible—"

“Unnecessary.” Square intercepted. “We will send a contingent to discuss the terms of our jointly-crewed mission. Please let any of us know if our assistance can be useful in the care of Lieutenant Keller.”

It seemed they had been dismissed.

HONORA III

✦ ✦ ✦

"I'm fine."

"No, you're not."

"Let us at least examine you."

"Fine," Lio exhaled the word more than said it. "I've never cut myself before. The knife just slipped out of my hand."

She still could not quite believe it. One moment she had been chopping vegetables, the next there was blood everywhere.

Rosa turned Lio's hand over, wiping away the blood again and again while watching her face more closely than the wound.

"Pregnancy exacts strange tolls on the body," she said, wrapping the cut in clean bandage. She held pressure longer than Lio thought necessary, then finally let go.

"Well," Lio muttered, "this one seems to want double."

Rosa's mouth twitched in amusement.

Thia stood by the door welcoming those who arrived for their celebration. Lio stayed to his side, accepting more hugs than she enjoyed, and allowing the others to fuss over her. Some brought carved toys for the twins. Others offered scraps of fabric, tiny blankets, or little drawings from eager children.

Rosa collected the gifts and arranged them on a nearby table beside the meal she had prepared and the small, decadent dessert reserved for special occasions.

Once everyone had settled, Thia and Lio lowered themselves onto worn cushions in the circle with the rest of the Seven. Older children read just outside the gathering while younger ones sat in the middle, playing with the same number games their parents once learned in the science center.

An empty cushion remained in the circle for Reve.

Some said it was tradition. Part of Doc's old command to stay together.

But for Lio, Reve was never symbolic.

She was simply still there.

Lio's gaze caught on the empty place. She felt her twin most sharply when they were all together, as if closeness made the absence louder.

Thia noticed and patted her hand lightly, pulling her attention back to the room.

Lio sighed and poked at the cake on her plate.

Rosa handed her a carved toy to occupy her hands. Lio turned it over absently, letting the warmth of voices around her blur into something soft and far away.

She was not ignorant of the glances. The quiet concern. The whispered comments she wasn't meant to hear.

Thia was right.

She was old.

The Seven shared a history woven thick with frays and knots, made beautiful only by the fact that it had held.

Lio's fingers stilled.

The carved toy suddenly felt heavy in her hand.

Her eyes drifted to the empty cushion.

For one suspended moment, she thought she saw a warm, indistinct glow resting there.

She blinked.

It was gone.

The winds were loud that night.

Lio lay awake beneath a mound of blankets, exhausted but unwilling to surrender to sleep. The cold had a way of creeping through even the best layers, and tonight it seemed to press at the walls harder than usual.

She shifted and felt something hard tumble against her wrist.

The carved toy.

Smiling faintly, she picked it up and turned it in her hand. The little stone figure reminded her of a robot from one of the books she loved as a child, the kind tucked deep in the science facility shelves.

"Ow—"

She dropped it into the blankets.

Her hand burned.

Not painfully, not exactly. Just enough to shock her fully awake.

She rubbed at her palm and squinted down at it. No blister. No mark. No heat remained.

Only the memory of it.

She stared at the toy.

Nothing.

Lio elbowed Thia harder than necessary.

He grunted and repositioned himself, but did not wake.

She pushed herself halfway upright—and the lights snapped on.

Lio flinched and fell back into the pillows, momentarily blinded.

“Come on,” she whispered harshly, shoving him again. “Don’t tell me you didn’t see that.”

Thia cracked one eye open and muttered something useless before drifting back toward sleep.

Lio grimaced at the sudden brightness, then at the stone figure resting innocently in the blankets.

By the time her eyes adjusted, the pull of sleep had returned, heavy and insistent.

“Never mind,” she grumbled, dragging the blankets back over herself.

But she didn’t sleep easily.

The autumn tempests raged across the surface for days after, their howling filtering down through the frozen city above. Most Honorans learned to live beneath the sound.

Lio never had.

To her, loud winds were a warning.

“You’re crying,” Rosa said softly. She set aside the blanket she had been folding and crossed the room. “What troubles you, sis—” She stopped then. Both of them flinched. For some reason, the word landed wrong.

Lio’s face crumpled. “It’s... it’s...” The rest dissolved into sobs.

She sank heavily onto a floor cushion and let the grief take her all at once, old and familiar and somehow fresh enough to hurt.

Rosa stood there for a moment, then quietly returned to the bed and resumed folding laundry with bowed head and deliberate hands.

It was the anniversary day Reve had not come back from the depths.

The door creaked open.

Cold air and the sound of the winds slipped in from the hall before Thia stepped through. The moment he saw Lio, he crossed to her without hesitation.

She didn't look up.

Her sobbing had slowed, but not stopped.

He looked to Rosa, but she kept her eyes on the linens.

"Nothing happened," she said before he could ask.

"Then why is she crying?"

Rosa opened her mouth, but Lio answered first.

"She called me sister."

The room went still.

Thia blinked once, then opened his mouth as if a useful answer might appear.

It didn't.

Finally he exhaled soundlessly and rubbed a hand over his beard.

"I don't understand," he said, "and maybe it's best if I don't get involved in this one."

He crossed to Rosa instead, kissed her forehead, and pulled her into a brief embrace. She sagged into him for only a moment before he let her go.

Then he grabbed one of the folded blankets from the bed.

The whole pile tipped over.

Rosa shut her eyes briefly, then bent to start folding them again.

Thia draped the salvaged blanket around Lio's shoulders and lowered himself beside her on the cushion. She leaned into him, staring down at her feet.

The glow was there again.

Faint. Warm. Pulsing between them.

Lio went still. She did not want to blink.

"What am I going to do with you?" Thia murmured tenderly.

Then he stiffened. His hand shot down between them and hit the floor.

Lio recoiled and stared at him.

"You... saw it?"

"I don't know," he said, too quickly. "I think so."

He looked at the space between them, then at her, then seemed to decide he wanted no part in whatever this was.

He kissed her temple and gave her shoulder a squeeze.

His voice was gentler when he said, "You should rest."

Lio gave him a small, crooked smile and pulled the blanket tighter around herself.

Thia stood and headed for the door.

His wives would sort this out better without him in the middle of it.

He reached the hall before realizing he had forgotten his gloves.

Behind him, the door creaked shut.

CHAPTER 14

Jo woke suddenly from an unsettling dream. She had a lingering sense of holding something, her fingers curved around a non-existent tool. She squeezed her eyes shut—the lighting on Tau never seemed to fade. Even at the darkest settings, light remained.

Giving up on sleep for now, she pulled on an exercise jumpsuit and shoes. Shaking out her arms and legs, she left the bedroom. Jo stood in the center of the common room. It felt hollow. Technically guest quarters, it made sense that there was no clutter or items displayed on the shelves. But this room was barren, as though not even dust had a place here.

She shivered and rubbed her arms. Little hairs on the back of her neck stood up. Leaving the room, she shielded her eyes. The light was much brighter in the hall compared to her room, she hadn't mentally prepared for it.

Turning right out of her doorway, Jo wandered the halls. Without direction markers it didn't seem to matter which way she went. The deck was circular, she'd get back eventually. Strolling along at a leisurely pace, the history of the station was evident. She saw wear marks that could not be smoothed, and grooves cut into the floor from repeated usage. Even the inset ladders on the walls had ancient finger grip marks. This was a station that had endured just as much as Epsilon.

Terrans and androids once lived on this station together. Then the Terrans left. They assumed the androids would carry on like automatons, handling tasks and charging low batteries. All they had to do was keep the station running and intercept... signals. She felt the clash of her assumptions and reality just then. Jo and her crew came here as though they commanded the station and all the androids in it, but was that never a possibility.

The floor was suddenly bathed in a much different light—Jo realized she had been looking at her feet most of the journey. Looking up she saw the vast algae ponds in their shrine-like setting. *Did they really have to grow so much of it?*

She was drawn to the incongruous sight of warm light and cold metal. Walking to the door, she was surprised when it opened. A small maintenance bot rolled out and beeped at her. The bot then raised two of its three fingers.

Peace?

Jo approached the bot with her own peace sign. It scooted out of the way, allowing her to pass into the room, then beeped at her three times before the door closed.

"Ah, you met Alpha-3-D," Sam said. Jo jumped, startled not realizing someone else was in the room.

"I, uh, yes? The bots have names?" She asked, wondering if everything on the station had a name.

"Well, I have not asked if it considers that a name, but that is the bot's designation. Given so we can take care of its maintenance needs, and retrieve it if stuck somewhere." It was clear they kept track of the station and its occupants. Sam turned back to the vat near the door, checking outputs on a datapad.

"Is there anything on the station you don't take care of?" Her tone was mildly sarcastic, but released some of the irritation Jo felt. She still couldn't reconcile how well the station operated without Terran presence. Weeks ago she was defending this very competency to Simmons and felt a pang of hypocrisy. She had an uneasy realization that they could be replaced on any of the stations.

"Oh, there are many things I do not take care of. That is why we have specialized roles." Sam said without looking up.

Jo sighed, suddenly regretting her walk. Sleeping under interminable lights was surely better than whatever this was.

"Was that not funny? Sensor often uses literal humor with me to dispel tension. Perhaps I did it wrong." Jo laughed, a bursting sound of delight. Everything she encountered here had been against her expectations. "No, you did it exactly right." She wiped a tear from the corner of her eye. Laughter had not come easily of late. Sam's mouth turned to smile, but her eyes narrowed at the same time. The comic relief was brief. "Why are you here, Jo Willis?"

"I couldn't sleep, so I went for a walk," Jo fidgeted with the cuff of her sleeve, feeling like that was the wrong answer. What was their insistence with using their full names all the time?

"I was unclear." Sam's voice was modulated for calm, but she didn't feel calm internally. "Why are you here, on Tau Station?"

"To ask for your help." *Wrong again.*

Jo took a deep breath and let it out slowly. She had to be transparent. Asking for their help was true, but it wasn't the reason. "We have a duty to respond to the distress call but not enough people to be successful."

"Ah," Sam replied, seeming to understand this practicality. "So is it only duty that drives you to respond?" Her question excited Jo, there was so much she wanted to see and experience.

"Well, no, I am also very interested in the planet and colony. I'd love to explore a new star system, and..." she trailed off seeing Sam change expressions.

Jo lowered her gaze, this feeling of being wrong all the time bothered her. She always had the answers, and here, on this station, she had none. Then she recalled Sam's words earlier: someone requested help and needs us. "You said back in the council that someone needs you. Is that what drives you? You care about them?"

"Is duty not care that has structure?"

Jo opened her mouth to respond, but no words came out. Duty as care?

It was not a concept she had considered before. Duty was something imposed—by rank, by law, by expectation. Care was something felt.

She had always believed the two were separate things. Sam seemed perfectly content to treat them as the same.

Jo was suddenly very warm and needed to sit down—she lowered herself to the floor. The grating was cold and uncomfortable even through her jumpsuit.

Sam regarded her quietly before sitting beside her. They sat together without speaking.

The algae vats hummed softly as pumps circulated the green water through the filtration channels. Light from the tanks washed across the metal walls in slow rippling patterns. The glow was warmer than the station lights outside, almost gentle.

Jo rested her elbows on her knees and watched the movement of the water.

Duty as care that has structure.

The words rolled through her mind again. If that was true, then everything she believed about this mission was wrong. She had told her crew they were coming to Tau because it was their duty.

She exhaled slowly.

Maybe she hadn't been as honest with herself as she thought. Neither of them spoke.

For the first time since arriving on Tau Station, Jo felt something loosen in her chest.

The question she had been avoiding was finally clear.

Why was she really here?

CHAPTER 15

On Tau Station, Jo wasn't the only one who couldn't sleep.

Simmons routed himself to one of the auxiliary training bays. The space was small, functional, and probably rarely used. A place meant for bodies, not meetings.

He keyed the lights higher than necessary. Habit. One designed to help him focus.

He set the resistance, tested the tension, reset it. Again, then started the set.

Pull. *Keller said she's fine.*

Release. *She knows I'm not stupid.*

Pull. *She's always "fine."*

Release. *When she needs me, she'll tell me.*

He focused on form. On breath. On the familiar burn in his shoulders. Motion organized his thoughts. It always had. He hoped it would tonight.

After several minutes he realized there were others in the room. Not his people.

Two androids were near the far wall. They weren't observing him. They weren't working. One was seated on the floor, back against the metal paneling. The other was adjusting something at the joint of its wrist with slow, careful movements. It studied the joint closely as it worked, delicate, careful.

He almost told them to clear the bay.

Security protocol. Controlled space. No loitering.

The words lined themselves up automatically.

Then stalled.

They weren't in the way.

They weren't interfering.

They weren't doing anything that fell under any category he had authority over.

They were simply... there. And he didn't have authority here.

Simmons resumed the set, harder this time. Faster. The controlled burn edged toward strain.

The seated android moved its head, watching the other's hand.

There was nothing to report.

Nothing to stop.

Nothing to secure.

He slowed. Then stopped altogether.

His hands remained on the grips long after the tension went slack.

He had thought the mission was about what waited at Honora.

What they would find. What they could save.

It wasn't.

It was about whether there was still anything, anyone left there to return. And to return unchanged.

He let go.

The machine did not reset itself.

Across the room, the androids continued exactly as they had been.

Simmons lowered himself onto the bench beside the frame. Not to rest.

Just because there was nowhere else to put what he was feeling.

Tau Station had not breached anything.

The breach had already happened.

And there was no position left to defend.

✦ ✦ ✦

Sam stood at the edge of vat seven. It was not on her schedule, she came here as if pulled by gravity.

The algae moved in slow, looping currents beneath the surface. Light from the overhead panels filtered through the liquid, diffused into a soft green glow. The movement should have been uniform. It was not.

She had reviewed the data logs repeatedly.

All values were within acceptable parameters.

They did not match what she observed.

Sam adjusted the display on her datapad, scrolling through the last several cycles. The numbers repeated in consistent intervals. Growth rate. Nutrient balance. Circulation flow.

Identical.

Behind her, the door opened with a soft mechanical release.

Sensor entered and paused just inside the threshold. He did not announce himself immediately. Sam had not reacted.

He noted the time.

"Sam," he said after a moment.

She did not turn. "Yes."

"You have been in this room for three cycles."

"I am aware."

He stepped closer, setting his tools on the nearby work surface. The temperature here was marginally elevated compared to the rest of the station. He adjusted his internal calibration.

"What are you observing?" he asked.

Sam angled the datapad toward him but did not look away from the vat.

"The readings are stable," she said. "They should not be."

Sensor reviewed the data.

"All values fall within expected ranges."

"Yes."

"That indicates correct function."

"Yes."

He paused.

"You disagree."

Sam's fingers tightened around the datapad.

"It does not feel correct."

Sensor agreed but needed more.

"Please define."

Sam hesitated.

"I can't."

He accepted this.

Sensor stepped forward until he stood beside her. Together they faced the vat.

The algae drifted in slow spirals. Occasionally, a current would shift, subtle but visible. Sensor tracked the motion.

He initiated a scan.

Circulation: stable. Temperature: stable. Growth: stable.

No anomaly detected.

He reached out and placed his hand lightly against the glass.

No change.

Sam lowered her datapad and did the same.

The algae shifted.

It was slight—barely perceptible—but immediate. A ripple passed through the vat, altering the pattern of movement. The spirals elongated, then tightened again.

Sensor checked the readings.

Growth variance: 3.1%.

He recalibrated.

Growth variance: 0%.

He ran the scan again.

Stable.

Sam withdrew her hand.

The movement settled.

"It is better now," she said.

Sensor looked at the data.
It was not better.
It was different.
He closed the log without saving.

HONORA IV

Lio stood in the science facility in front of a pile of medical texts on an otherwise empty table. *Folate, Vitamin B-12, Iron.* She sighed, these were the hardest to get, but the most essential nutrients for her and the twins. What was she going to do?

"Work the problem, Lio." That's what Doc would say. There was no use moping about it. "A bad solution was better than no solution." She closed her eyes for a moment and set about her work again. Lio flipped through the pages of the pharmacology texts carefully searching for inspiration. There was a section in Alternative Nutrition about a thing called "algae" that looked interesting. That contained all of these nutrients and more. But where would she get that on a frozen planet? Tears formed in the corner of her eyes but refused to fall.

"I need you—"

“And here I am.” She shook her head. Thia. Always there at the exact right or wrong time. He placed his hands lightly on her shoulders and kissed the top of her head.

“Doc, I need Doc,” she whispered. He made a sort of grunting acknowledgement, maybe disappointed she hadn’t said his name instead.

Releasing her gently, Thia turned to the shelves. Not needing to be asked. Most of the books had been moved to the Seven’s homes, but some remained in the science facility. No one really wanted “A Treatise on Atmospheric Particulates” as bedtime reading.

“What are we looking for?” He asked without much curiosity.

“Looking for something to help me with these babies. But if you find a worn out book about robots, grab it,” she said hoping he really would find that one. The shelves did not contain much that seemed useful, but he worked more with his hands than his mind. He moved books around looking at the titles, putting them in loose stacks.

One stood out as not belonging with the others. The cover was worn but not in the usual way, and no pictures of robots.

He opened it, his eyes widened, and then he nearly dropped it. The book was not a book at all. Inside, the pages had been cut out in such a way that it still appeared solid. Within the hollowed out section was, oddly, another book. Small, looked like a journal. Mesmerized, he took it out carefully and flipped to a random page.

He only read a single line before closing the book within a book. Not wanting anyone else to see it, he buried it far behind the others. Returning to Lio's side, he joined her in looking through the books she laid out on the table.

"Anything interesting?" She asked, leaning against him.

"No, nothing at all." He said with a disinterested tone. He turned his head to look back at the pile that secretly contained the mysterious notebook. The line would be burned in his memory forever.

It simply said, "they can never know."

Chapter 16

Keller and Simmons were in their guest quarters—he thought it was weird they understood cohabitation. A larger room was provided for the two of them without question. Keller sat at the narrow table by the wall, a soft light panel was open in front of her. A checklist hovered above it, lines ticking green as she moved through them. Clothing allocations. Med kit verification. Water ration requests. Climbing gear.

Simmons sat on the couch behind her, elbows on his knees, hands loosely clasped. He had been staring at the floor longer than he meant to.

"Jan," he said.

"Hm?" She didn't look up, fingers still moving.

"I want to talk to you."

"Just a minute, Ace." She scrolled. "I'm almost—"

"Jan, please. I'm trying to talk to you."

"Ok, I said just a minute."

"I'm not going."

She nodded fractionally, distracted. "To dinner? They're expecting us."

"No," he said. His voice was steady, but it landed wrong in the room. He cleared his throat once. "I'm not going. That's what I'm trying to tell you."

Keller's hand stilled. The checklist dimmed where her finger hovered.

Slowly, she turned in her chair.

Simmons lifted his eyes to hers. He wasn't smiling. But he wasn't wrecked either. He looked... resolved. Tired. Like someone who had been awake all night and finally stopped arguing with himself.

"I'm not going to Honora."

For a moment, the room felt too quiet. Even Tau's low mechanical hum seemed to recede.

Keller searched his face for something else—a joke, a caveat, a correction.

"You—" she started, then stopped. "What do you mean, you're not going?"

"I mean I'm not getting on that ship."

Her mouth opened, closed. She pushed her chair back, as if she needed space just to breathe.

"You've been on the crew since the beginning," she said. "You planned the mission."

"I know."

"You told Jo you were in."

"I was."

"And now you're just... not?"

He exhaled through his nose, a short breath. "I didn't say 'just.'"

She stood. The checklist winked out, forgotten.

"This is because of Tau, isn't it?" she said. "Because of them."

"Partly."

"Partly," she echoed, incredulous. "Ace, we finally know where the Signal came from. We finally know there are people out there. We are days away from actually doing something about it and you're telling me you're going to stay on an empty station with androids and wall-bots?"

"With a functioning Quantcomm hub," he said quietly. "With the only deep-space relay between Epsilon and whatever comes next.

With the ones who are going to be coordinating everything once you're gone."

She shook her head. "They can send someone else."

"They already did," he said. "They sent you."

That landed harder than he meant it to.

Keller crossed her arms, more to hold herself together than defensively. "So that's it? You're staying... with them."

She looked away.

"Search and rescue can go wrong. You might need more than what you took. Someone might need to send ships after yours," he continued. "Supplies. Crews. Medical. Engineering. Whatever the Honorans ex-fil needs once you tell us what you find. Someone has to stay and coordinate"

"That doesn't have to be you."

"It does to me."

She laughed once, sharp and disbelieving. "So you're volunteering to be left behind."

"I'm choosing to be where I'm useful."

Keller's throat tightened. "You're useful with me."

His jaw flexed. "That's not in question."

Silence stretched between them.

Another long pause.

“And what about us?” she asked.

That was the question under all the others.

He stood then, slow, careful, like he didn’t want to startle her.

“I’m not leaving you,” he said. “I’m staying in the last place you can still come back to.”

Her breath hitched despite her.

“That’s not comforting,” she whispered.

“I know.”

HONORA V

On the underground path between the living areas and the science facility, Lio took the hewn stone steps to the lower level.

Her hip joint popped, relieving strain. She felt old and chuckled to herself—there's a reason babies are for the young. Her bones hurt in ways she didn't remember from before.

Asha had been an easy baby. Lio was never sick or had to slow down. Asha was even born easy, a rare gift on Honora. Lio pressed a palm against a carved handhold to stabilize herself. Her breath caught at the unexpected remembrance. Her firstborn had not survived the birth of her own first child.

What was it Rosa had said? *Pregnancy exacts strange tolls...*

Life here could be harsh, cruel even. Naturally they took in her son, Aja, and raised him alongside hers and Rosa's. Not that children of

Honora were limited to family by birth--they were all a family. It was how things were done.

A light flickered down the hall. Lio's heart skipped a beat. She grabbed the smooth stone handle, eyes closed momentarily against the discomfort in her chest. *How are they going to get me down here when it's time?* Feeling physically, if not emotionally, steadier she finished the short steps to the next level.

Again, the light dimmed and brightened suddenly--the surprise making her heart flutter once more. She heard a ghost, "Too much strain on your heart, little lion." *Yeah, and I should probably drink more water too, huh, Doc?* The ghost was silent after that.

Making her way gingerly down the hall, Lio figured out the light wasn't flickering. It was being blocked. *What is Thia...* She shook her head, not wanting to know. This wasn't her stop anyway—but curiosity wouldn't let her keep walking.

"Thia, aren't you supposed to be in the rear tunnel?" She called to him across the room.

"Ah, I had Aja cover my route today." Lio grimaced, her head bowed at the name of her foster son.

"What is it?" He climbed down from his tinkering, concerned.

"I—it's nothing..." Nothing she wanted to talk about right now.

"I'm just going to keep asking until you tell me." He smiled in that way she knew he meant it.

"What are *you* doing in here?" Two could play this game.

"I was..." he paused and she raised her eyebrows, "fixing this." He gestured vaguely over his shoulder at the light and the paneling around it. She narrowed her eyes at him.

"You weren't. But that's fine." She waved it off. She exhaled heavily, rubbing her belly. "I was..." she started out imitating his phrasing, "Asha." Her face fell and she crumpled against him.

Thia wrapped his large body around her like he could hold her together. Grief was a part of life for the Seven. Asha was their light in the dark. Lio said her name less as the years went on—but she was never loved less. After a while, Lio's hip began to hurt again and she pushed him away lightly, squeezing his hand before letting go. She turned to go back to the hall, and her task. "Why are *you* down here?" He asked gently.

She turned to look at him square on. Calm, resolved. "We need to be ready."

"Ready for what?"

He didn't know.

That was the problem.

"In case I can't get down here in time. For the twins." She didn't look at him when she said it. The thought didn't go away. It didn't need to.

Understanding dawned on his face, Thia was emphatic, "Of course we'll make it. We'll carry you if we have to." He wanted good plans to be good enough.

"Necessity exists, Thia." She said and left the room.

Thia frowned at that.

He had heard it before. Before bad things happened.

In the corridor, Lio paused at the top of the steps, one hand braced against the wall.

The distance down felt longer than it had before.

Chapter 17

Jo carried multiple data pads toward the loading bay, shifting their weight in her arms as she walked. Instead of taking the most direct route, she detoured through the algae decks.

It had become a habit.

The quiet, humid warmth of the vats offered something the rest of the station did not—a sense of life that was steady, contained, and indifferent to everything else happening around it. She paused for only a moment this time, letting her gaze drift across the softly lit water before moving on.

They were leaving.

And still, there were details to check.

Each data pad held a different manifest—equipment, personnel, research allocations—organized so she could track each process group without overlap. As she flipped between them, her attention snagged on the archaeology list.

Too short.

She tapped her foot absently.

What were they missing? Materials? Or had no one expected there to be anything worth studying?

She made a mental note to ask Keller.

The loading bay doors opened as she approached.

She assumed they had opened for her.

They had not.

She walked directly into Sensor.

The impact sent several data pads clattering across the deck, the sharp sound echoing through the otherwise quiet corridor.

"—oh!" Jo dropped to her knees to gather them.

Sensor did the same.

They bumped heads.

"Ow!"

They both said it at the same time.

For a moment, they stared at each other.

Then laughed.

Jo rubbed her forehead lightly. "Why did you say 'ow'?"

Sensor tilted his head. "Why did you?"

She paused, still half-crouched on the floor, considering the question more seriously than she expected to.

"When our heads collided, I was surprised," she said slowly. "It's... a signal, I think. A way to indicate that something potentially injurious just happened."

"But you were not injured."

"I don't think so."

"Then the exclamation is not for pain."

Jo blinked. "Not exactly. More like... a reflex. It tells others I might need help. Even if I don't."

Sensor looked up and away, as if confirming a hypothesis.

"I have been practicing Terran mannerisms," he said. "This was useful data."

Jo closed her eyes briefly and shook her head. "That's... unsettling."

He handed her the last of the datapads.

"May I ask about your plans for the loading bay?"

She stood, shifting back into motion. "I'm reviewing manifests. Again. I could use a fresh set of eyes on this—if you're available."

"That may prove difficult," he replied. "I have not had fresh eyes in at least a hundred cycles."

Jo laughed.

"Sam told me you were funny."

A small, unmistakable grin crossed Sensor's face as he accepted the data pad she handed him.

The practiced ease of the exchange should have settled her.

It didn't.

Because there was still one conversation she hadn't had yet.

✦ ✦ ✦

Jo found him in one of the auxiliary cargo prep rooms two hours before departure.

Not because he was hard to find.

Because he was exactly where someone went when they didn't want to be in the places everyone else would expect them.

The room was half-lit, quiet except for the low refrigeration hum from the adjacent storage lockers. A stack of sealed equipment bins sat open on one of the worktables, none of them being worked on. Simmons stood beside them with a manifest pad in one hand and no visible interest in the numbers.

He looked up when she entered.

No surprise.

That irritated her immediately.

"Commander," he said.

Jo let the door close behind her.

"I'm told you're no longer on my departure roster."

Not a question.

Simmons set the pad down. "Yes, ma'am."

Jo watched him for a moment.

Whatever argument he'd had with himself was already over.

She folded her arms.

"You were planning to tell me personally?"

"Yes."

A beat.

"When?"

He didn't answer fast enough.

"Helpful." She was not going to make this easy.

"I should have come to you sooner," he said.

"Yes," Jo replied. "You should have."

Silence, brief and edged.

"You want to explain why my security officer is pulling himself off a first-contact mission two hours before departure?"

Simmons exhaled through his nose.

"Because I'm more useful here."

Jo didn't move. "That's the polished version. Try the one underneath."

His jaw tightened.

"For a mission like this," he said, "you don't come back the same."

Jo held his gaze. She'd heard that before.

He continued before she could respond.

"I thought we were recovering survivors. Assessing, stabilizing. But that's not what this is."

"No?" Jo said.

"No."

The room felt smaller.

Jo didn't disagree. She just kept moving anyway.

"What do you think it is?"

A beat.

"A threshold."

Jo almost smiled.

Not because it was funny.

Because it was precise.

Simmons saw it too and flattened it immediately.

"I don't think this stops at coordinates and atmosphere," he said. "I think it changes people just by being real."

Jo let that sit.

“And your response to that,” she said, “is to remain at the relay station.”

“No, ma’am.”

“No?”

“My response is to stay where I can still do the part I know I can do.”

Better.

Still not the whole truth.

“You understand,” Jo said, “that if you’d reached this conclusion three days ago, I could have built around it.”

“Yes, ma’am.”

“A week ago, I could have requested a replacement.”

“Yes, ma’am.”

“Before I finalized my team, I could have respected it.”

That one landed.

Simmons looked down—briefly—then back up.

“That’s fair.”

“I’m not interested in fair,” Jo said. “I’m interested in not having my mission shift under me two hours before departure.”

He absorbed that without flinching.

“I’ve already transferred remote security protocols,” he said. “Emergency routing, cargo locks, hangar response, relay failover. Chen has shipboard control. I can coordinate from here."

Jo didn't answer immediately.

Because he wasn't wrong.

Which made this worse.

"Do you want me to talk you out of it?" she asked.

He blinked, caught off guard.

"No, ma'am."

"Good. I wasn't going to."

She stepped closer, glanced at the manifest.

Real work. Useful work.

Not the work he'd agreed to do.

"You staying here may be useful," she said. "I'm not arguing that."

He said nothing.

"But usefulness is not the same thing as courage."

Simmons didn't respond.

There wasn't time.

The mission had already moved past him.

Silence.

The refrigeration unit hummed softly.

He met her gaze.

"I know."

No defense. No excuse.

Just truth.

Jo found she respected that more than she wanted to.

Not enough to like this.

Enough not to despise him.

She straightened.

“Keller knows?”

“Yes.”

“How bad?”

He looked away.

“Bad enough.”

“That sounds accurate.”

A beat.

“You will be present for departure.”

His eyes lifted immediately.

Not surprise.

Something closer to dread.

Jo didn’t soften.

“You don’t get to remove yourself from the consequences of your decision. If you stay, you stay visibly.”

For a moment, he almost argued.

Then didn’t.

“Yes, ma’am.”

Jo moved to the door, then stopped.

Without turning:

“For what it’s worth, Lieutenant—”

He straightened.

She looked back over her shoulder.

"I don't think you're wrong."

That hit.

She let it, and took a longer beat than necessary before adding, "I think you're early."

And left him with it.

✦ ✦ ✦

Simmons was where Jo had ordered him to be.

That did not make it easier.

The staging hangar was louder than usual, not because anyone was speaking above regulation level but because departure always made ordinary sound feel temporary. Cargo locks cycling. Cart wheels over deck seams. final checks called across short distances. The kind of motion that meant people had already committed to leaving, whether or not they were ready.

He stood off to one side of the loading corridor in station uniform rather than field gear.

That alone felt like a confession.

No one said anything to him directly.

Which was worse.

Chen bobbed his head once when he passed with a crate balanced against one shoulder.

An acknowledgment, nothing more or less.

Najma crossed the hangar without looking at him at all.

One of the maintenance bots rolled between cargo stacks dragging a cable spool and nearly clipped his boot. He stepped back automatically.

Across the open bay, Keller was running final comm checks with one side of her headset off, datapad braced against her forearm. Efficient. Focused. Entirely occupied.

She didn't look at him.

Not once.

That was fair.

More than fair.

The ship sat beyond her with its loading ramp still extended, lights running low along the seam.

Open.

Waiting.

Simmons had spent enough years around deployment staging to know that once a ship looked like that, it already belonged more to the people boarding it than the people left behind.

He wondered, distantly, if that was always true of thresholds.

That once crossed, they stopped being about the ones who stayed.

"Lieutenant."

He turned.

Jo stood a few paces away, hands clasped behind her back, gaze flicking once toward the boarding ramp and then back to him.

No wasted movement, no wasted sympathy.

"Commander."

"We're green."

He nodded. "Relay remains green on this side. Comm routing is stable. I'll monitor for burst lag and signal degradation through the first transit window."

Jo held his gaze for one second longer than necessary.

Not because she doubted the work.

Because she wanted him to stand in it.

Then she said, "Good."

That was all.

No closure.

No forgiveness.

No ceremonial exchange of responsibility.

Just command acknowledging function.

And moving on.

Jo turned away before he could think of anything useful or useless to add.

That was fair too.

A final departure call sounded across the hangar.

Movement sharpened immediately.

Crew converged.

Cases lifted.

The loose edges of the room pulled into purpose.

Keller crossed the floor toward the boarding line without looking left or right.

For one stupid second Simmons thought she might still turn.

She didn't.

Of course she didn't.

He watched her hand the datapad off, adjust the strap on her field bag, and step up the ramp without once glancing back toward the station side of the bay.

Then she was gone into the ship.

The ramp stayed open another thirty seconds.

Maybe less.

Long enough to make him understand exactly what Jo had meant.

Visible.

Present.

Here.

When the ramp finally began to lift, Simmons felt the movement in his chest before he registered it with his eyes. Once the final clearance came through, there was no longer a version of this mission that included everyone who had started it.

The seam closed.

The lights shifted.

The ship ceased to be a place people could still choose.

And then it was only machinery again.

A vessel.

A mission.

A direction he had not taken.

The hangar grew quieter in pieces.

Not silence.

Just aftermath.

Simmons stood where he was until the launch clamps released and the ship eased free of the station with a force so controlled it almost looked gentle.

Almost.

He watched until the external bay doors cycled and the ship was gone.

Only then did he let himself exhale.

Not relief.

Not regret exactly.

Something harder to name.

The shape of a life continuing after a line had already been crossed.

Behind him, Tau Station kept humming.

Waiting.

Still here.

And for better or worse, so was he.

CHAPTER 18

There was no ceremony.

No speech. No gathering.

The Terran and Tau crews boarded the ship quietly, the last of the crates already secured. When they paused at the base of the loading ramp, it was not out of ritual, but because there was nothing left to do.

The bay felt smaller now.

Empty.

Jo turned to the androids. "Would you like to close the airlock?"

It was a small gesture, but it felt appropriate.

The crew nominated Sam.

She accepted.

They waited.

The moment stretched.

Sam stood at the control panel, hand poised.

She did not press the button.

Not immediately.

Jo felt the pause before she understood it. A subtle tension moved through the group—uncertain, then noticeable.

Press it, Sam.

For a moment, Jo wasn't sure if she had thought it... or if it had simply occurred.

The control panel glowed green.

Jo was suddenly unsure whether any meaningful amount of time had passed at all.

Then, in a blink, the airlock cycled.

The delay vanished as quickly as it had appeared.

Jo exhaled slowly.

Perhaps she had imagined it.

As the doors sealed, she glanced around.

The others were gone.

Only she and Sam remained.

That didn't feel right.

The ship departed without ceremony.

✦ ✦ ✦

Jo stood in the corridor outside the bridge, one hand resting lightly against the bulkhead as the drive engaged. There was no dramatic shift—only a subtle recalibration, the stars beyond the viewport rearranging themselves into unfamiliar constellations.

"Transit confirmed," Evan's voice came over the intercom.

Calm. Controlled.

Almost indifferent.

That was it.

No acknowledgment. No gathering.

No one marking the moment.

Jo pushed off the wall and walked on, the ship felt normal.

Too normal.

Doors closed. Systems hummed. Someone laughed somewhere out of sight. Water ran through pipes.

Life continued.

Unchanged.

This should feel bigger.

They were crossing interstellar space with a mixed crew, responding to a signal no one else had answered.

That should mean something.

She checked the observation deck.

Empty.

Not abandoned.

Just... unused.

The space had been designed for people to gather. To witness.

No one was there.

Jo stood for a moment, looking out at the stars as they slipped past.

A quiet thought settled in.

If no one is here to see this... does it matter that we're doing it?

She shook her head.

Science did not require ceremony.

It required observation.

And suddenly—

she was very aware of how few of them were actually watching. The absence settled into the ship faster than anyone acknowledged.

Jo carried it with her anyway.

Jo woke in a cold sweat in the commander's quarters.

Her shirt clung to her skin, damp and uncomfortable. The room was quiet. Still. Nothing out of place.

She swung her legs over the side of the bed.

The moment her bare foot touched the cold metal floor—

everything changed.

She stood in a city.

Or what remained of one.

Ice climbed the skeletal remains of buildings, clinging to twisted structures that reached upward like something grown rather than built. The sky above was a flat, ashen gray.

She stepped forward.

The shards beneath her feet should have cut her.

They did not.

She was not there.

But the sound—

It was there.

A cry. The cry from her dreams.

Everywhere.

It moved through the hollow spaces, shifting as she turned. Louder. Sharper. More defined.

Not a cry.

The Signal.

Chapter 19

✦ ✦ ✦

The narrow corridor of the *Viga* still smelled faintly of solvent and machine oil as Jo entered the common room.

It was immediately obvious the space had not been designed for all of them at once. The table was too small, the seating too narrow, the lighting tuned for alertness rather than comfort—a room meant for rotation, not gathering.

They gathered anyway.

Jo sat with one boot hooked under the table, tray offset in front of her. Keller leaned back from the edge, cup in hand but untouched. Evan had claimed space by sheer persistence, and Chip occupied what remained as if it had been assigned to him personally.

Najma sat near the wall, angled just enough to suggest she might leave. Sam and Sensor took the last available space without contributing to the crowding, which Sensor had begun to suspect was not accidental.

Seven bodies in a space built for five.

No one mentioned it.

Chip was speaking.

"—and I'm telling you, if the storage bins had been arranged by anyone with even a passing relationship to spatial reasoning, this would not be an issue."

"It is not an issue," Keller said.

"It is an unfolding injustice."

"It is a preference."

"It is a betrayal of symmetry."

Evan laughed, mouth still half full.

Jo didn't look up. "You're going to have to choose which of those you believe."

"All of them," Chip said.

"That's not how belief works."

"That's exactly how belief works."

Najma smiled into her cup.

The expression landed a beat late.

Sensor noticed.

Jo answered too quickly. Evan spoke over her, then stopped. Keller began a response and didn't finish it.

The conversation didn't collapse.

It failed to resolve.

Then the room went quiet.

Not abruptly. Not completely. Just... all at once.

Evan looked up from his tray. Keller's grip tightened on the cup. Jo made a face—not at anyone, but at the absence of continuation. Chip's expression shifted from amusement to something closer to suspicion.

Sam did not move.

That was how Sensor knew she felt it too.

Evan broke first.

"...okay," he said. "That was strange."

Chip pointed at him immediately. "Yes. Thank you."

Jo looked around the table. "No, it was."

"What was?" Najma asked.

"That." Jo gestured vaguely between them. "We just... stopped."

"We paused," Keller said.

"No. Not like that."

The overhead lights dimmed briefly, then corrected.

This time Keller noticed first. Her eyes flicked upward—and she said nothing.

That was more telling than if she had.

"Okay," Jo said quietly. "No. That one was worse."

“What one?” Evan asked.

She didn’t answer right away, “I don’t know.”

No one helped her.

That irritated her.

“I was about to say something,” she said.

“You were,” Najma said.

Jo turned toward her. “Did you know what it was?”

“No.”

Chip raised one hand. “I would like it noted that this room is becoming increasingly hostile to communication.”

“That is because you are in it,” Keller said.

“Rude.”

Evan laughed.

Too early.

He stopped immediately.

This time no one missed it.

No one was eating anymore. Nothing visible had changed—and yet the room had become difficult to occupy. Not dangerous. Not unstable.

Resistant.

Jo looked at Sensor. “You’re doing it again.”

He blinked once. “Doing what?”

“The thing where you’ve already decided something and are debating whether to tell us.”

Chip laughed. "That is his default state."

Sensor ignored him.

Jo did not, "what is it?"

He considered not answering.

Across from him, Sam lifted her cup. She didn't drink. He found that to be unhelpful in deciding what to say.

"It may be environmental," he said.

That was enough.

Keller leaned forward alert, maybe concerned. "Environmental how?"

Sensor should not have looked at Sam.

He did. She was watching the table—not the people, the pattern.

He returned his attention to Keller.

"The timing of your interactions has been inconsistent."

Evan stared at him. "That is a wild sentence."

"It is also correct."

"Based on what?"

"Interruption frequency. Response latency. Transfer hesitation."

"You mean we're talking weird," Evan said.

"Yes," Sensor said. "With structure."

Chip thumped the table. "I hate that phrasing."

Keller didn't.

"And you think the room is influencing that," she said.

Closer now. More precise.

Sensor answered too slowly.

Jo noticed. Of course she did.

"You do," she said.

The ventilation shifted overhead with a soft, contained hiss.

No one spoke. Not immediately.

Then Sam said, quietly, "I think some environments stop being neutral once enough people begin trying to mean things inside them."

The sentence did not clarify anything.

Evan looked like he wanted to laugh and decided not to. Chip scowled at the table. Najma went still, as if listening inward rather than outward. Keller looked interested.

Jo looked dissatisfied.

"What does that mean?" she asked.

Sam's gaze remained on the table. "At minimum, that proximity is not passive."

No one moved.

Chip exhaled. "No. Don't like that."

That broke something loose.

Evan laughed—this time at the correct moment. Keller followed. Jo did too, briefly.

The rhythm returned.

Not fully.

Enough.

Sensor noticed Sam notice it. She reached for her utensil.

"You approve?" he asked quietly.

"No," she said. "I'm observing what it required."

That stayed with him. Because she was right.

Whatever this was, it was not only altering systems—it was changing effort. What it took to align. What it took to misfire.

When the group dispersed, it happened without coordination. Trays cleared, chairs shifted, bodies redistributed.

At the end, only Sam and Sensor remained.

The room looked smaller while empty.

Sensor stood beside the table longer than necessary.

"You are doing it again," Sam said.

"Doing what?"

"Trying to isolate something that is no longer behaving in isolation."

He exhaled. "That is an irritating sentence."

"I know."

He looked at the table, then the room, then the absence of everyone who had filled it.

"You think this followed us."

Sam was quiet for a moment.

"No," she said. "I think it was waiting for enough of us to notice it."

That was worse.

He did not say so.

They left without mentioning the subtle shift in airflow as the door closed behind them.

Chapter 20

Keller found Jo in the environmental prep bay two hours before transit exit.

The room was narrow and overlit, built for efficiency rather than comfort. Suit racks lined one wall in precise intervals, while open storage bins sat half-filled with field kits, med packs, sensor tabs, spare filters—the hundred small things that only became catastrophes after someone forgot them.

Jo stood at the central work surface with a checklist open on one datapad and a partially assembled environmental kit spread in front of her.

Keller paused in the doorway for a moment, then stepped inside.

Jo looked up immediately. "Please tell me you're here to confirm we packed enough adapters."

"No," Keller said. "Though I respect the attempt."

Jo huffed a quiet laugh and returned to the kit. "That's unfortunate. I was hoping for an easy conversation."

Keller set her crate down on the adjacent counter. "Then I'm definitely in the wrong room."

Jo sealed a case with more force than necessary. "Good. At least we're aligned on something."

For a minute, they worked in parallel—packaging seals, datapad taps, the low mechanical hum of the ship filling the space between them.

It would have been easy to leave it there.

That was probably why Jo didn't.

"You've been thinking loudly for hours," she said without looking up. "You may as well just say it."

Keller glanced over. "Is that how you experience me?"

"Unfortunately, yes."

"That seems inefficient."

Jo smiled, recalling the android's phrasing. "You've been spending too much time around Sensor."

"I have."

The smile faded as quickly as it came.

Keller recognized the shift. Jo had already made a decision—she just hadn't said it out loud yet.

That made this easier.

"I don't think we know what kind of situation we're entering," Keller said.

Jo didn't answer immediately. She moved one sealed case aside and reached for the next, as if the sequence of tasks suddenly mattered more than the conversation.

"We know enough," she said at last.

"That's not what I said."

Jo looked up then.

No irritation. No sharpness.

Just attention.

Keller didn't give her time to reframe it.

"We're preparing like this is a distress environment," she said, gesturing lightly to the open kits between them. "System failure. Survivors in crisis."

"We are."

"Maybe."

Jo leaned one hand against the work surface. "Keller—"

"No. Listen for a second."

Jo went still.

That was enough.

Keller set the filter down and rested both hands on the counter.

"The Signal told us someone wanted to be heard," she said. "It didn't tell us what kind of world they built while no one was listening."

The words held.

Jo didn't dismiss them.

She rarely did.

"We've already seen Tau change under isolation," Keller continued. "Not just structurally—socially. Behaviorally. If Tau adapted, then Honora almost certainly did too."

Jo looked down at the med kit between them.

"Adaptation doesn't erase harm," she said. "Surviving something doesn't make it acceptable."

"True."

Jo exhaled slowly. "That's the problem."

Keller waited.

"When the Signal arrived," Jo said, "I thought we were dealing with something terrible but legible. A damaged colony. Survivors. A system we could assess."

"And now?"

Jo didn't hesitate.

"Now I think it's worse than that."

Keller was unconvinced. "Worse how?"

"As in prolonged isolation. Environmental instability. Cultural drift under closed conditions." She looked up. "A place can be livable and still be intolerable."

There it was. The shape of the decision Jo had already made.

Keller felt it settle. Compassion--sharpened into certainty--which made it dangerous.

"Yes," Keller said. "It can."

Jo held her gaze, waiting.

Keller didn't soften it.

"But coherence still matters," she said. "Because if we mistake adaptation for damage, then every decision we make after that is built on the wrong premise."

Silence stretched between them. The ship gave a low, nearly sub-audible shift as internal systems adjusted for the coming deceleration burn. They knew the transit exit was getting closer.

Jo looked past Keller toward the sealed prep bay door.

"What are you asking me to do?" she said quietly.

Keller rubbed her neck, that was the most Jo question possible.

Not *are you right?* Not *what do you mean?*

Simply, what action follows from uncertainty?

"I'm not saying we should turn around," Keller said.

Jo's shoulders loosened, her expression didn't.

"I'm asking you not to decide in advance what helping is going to look like."

Jo said nothing.

Keller pushed once more.

"We keep using rescue language," she said. "Assessment. Viability. Extraction. Stabilization." She shook her head. "Those are Terran categories. They may not describe what's actually there."

Jo looked down at the equipment between them. It was all ordered, rational, and built for response.

"But that's the mission we agreed on," she said. "What would you call it instead?"

Keller considered that, then answered honestly.

"I don't know."

Jo gave a short, humorless laugh. "That's not very useful."

"No," Keller said. "It's just accurate."

Jo sighed and picked up the datapad again—not because the conversation was over, but because she needed something procedural to hold onto.

"When we get there," she said, scanning the checklist without reading it, "we still have to make judgments."

"I know."

"We can't just arrive and refuse to interpret what we're seeing."

"I know."

Jo looked up.

"And if it's as bad as I think it might be?"

There it was. Not authority. Not control. Fear.

Keller softened, but not enough to let her off the hook.

"Then we respond to what's actually there," she said. "Not to what we expected to find."

Jo held her gaze for a long moment. Then nodded once, it was small and controlled, but there.

"I can do that."

Keller believed her.

That was the trouble. Because Jo probably could—right up until the moment duty hardened again.

It was something.

Keller closed the last latch and slid the crate back toward the wall. The ship's internal comm chimed softly overhead. Transit exit in ninety minutes. Final prep in thirty.

Neither of them moved at first.

Then Jo exhaled and reached for the next pack.

"We should finish this."

"Probably."

They went back to work.

Not because the conversation had resolved anything.

Because the ship was still moving.

Because Honora was still ahead of them.

Because whatever waited there had already existed long enough to survive without their understanding of it.

✦ ✦ ✦

Exiting the corridor to Honoran space was, at first glance, unremarkable.

The stars stretched across the view screen as the ship translated, a familiar distortion that resolved itself in seconds. Then they were still again—fixed points of light against a dark that felt deeper than before. The ship's systems adjusted without comment, as they always did.

For a moment, no one reacted.

It was the kind of transition they had performed several times on this route. Routine. Predictable.

A chime sounded from the shipboard computer.

It came a beat too late.

The delay was small—barely noticeable—but it lingered in the quiet that followed, as though something had hesitated before acknowledging their arrival.

A kind of lethargy had settled over the crew during the long journey. Months in transit had softened their edges. Reactions were slower, conversations quieter. Even excitement had dulled into something more measured.

Still, this felt... off.

Sam watched Evan from her station.

His hand hovered over the intercom control, suspended just above the surface. She tracked the pause automatically, her internal clock marking the interval with precision.

It extended beyond what was necessary.

Beyond what was typical.

She shifted her attention, not outward but laterally.

Sensor had already noticed.

He did not turn immediately, but there was a subtle change in his posture—an alignment of attention that mirrored her own. When he finally glanced in her direction, it was brief. Enough to confirm.

Something is wrong.

Evan's hand dropped to the control with more force than required.

"Yes, bridge?" Jo's voice came through, steady and composed, though she had not expected the call.

"Ah—uh—we have entered the Honoran system, Commander."

The words were correct.

The tone was not.

Flat. Muted. Stripped of the usual spark that accompanied first arrival in a new system. None of his enthusiasm from being on Tau Station.

Sam studied him for a moment longer. The Terrans often required additional rest during extended missions. Their biological systems were not as resilient. Fatigue, stress—these were common.

This did not match those patterns.

Sensor met her gaze again, his head angling in a gesture that had become familiar between them.

Acknowledgment.

"On my way," Jo replied, and the line went quiet.

Before the interruption, Jo had been reviewing Honora's planetary systems—or what remained of them.

The colony ship still held orbit, though only just. Its trajectory had degraded over time, a slow decay that would eventually end in atmospheric entry. A century, perhaps. Less, if conditions shifted.

It responded to her pings, but only minimally. Acceptance packets returned with mechanical consistency, devoid of meaningful data.

She stared unhappily at the screen.

Not because she expected a fully operational vessel.

Because she had hoped for it.

The planet below offered little encouragement.

Ice covered most of the visible landmasses, broken only by dark fractures of water where the oceans still moved. Even that motion was tenuous, maintained by tidal forces from the system's outer moon. Without it, the planet would have frozen entirely—an inert sphere of ice drifting along its orbit of the central star.

What a miserable place.

Jo adjusted the atmospheric models, watching the projections shift across her display. Wind patterns were extreme but consistent, cycling with a regularity that suggested predictability with enough data.

If she could identify the pattern, she could find a window.

They would need one.

Pling.

The soft tone cut through her concentration.

A response had come from the surface.

She straightened, scanning the incoming data. One of the surface interception modules was still active—barely, but enough to respond.

Jo sent an authorization code, fingers moving quickly across the interface. They did not need a defensive system mistaking them for a threat.

She waited.

A moment stretched.

Then—

Authorization granted.

She let out a quiet breath she hadn't realized she was holding.

At least that part would not be a problem.

By the time Jo reached the bridge, the others had already gathered.

Keller stood near the main display, arms folded, her gaze fixed on the surface readouts. Evan remained at his station, though he seemed less settled than usual. Sam and Sensor stood apart, but only just, their attention divided between the data and the people interpreting it. Najma watched everything.

The display resolved into a single point of interest.

A faint but concentrated heat signature beneath the surface.

Small.

Stable.

Alive.

"Settlement," Keller said, more to confirm the thought than to introduce it.

"Underground," Jo replied, stepping forward. "Has to be."

Silence followed—not uncertainty, but calculation. Each of them was already running through possibilities, constraints, risks.

Landing would be the problem.

Too far from the site, and they would be forced to cross open terrain in extreme cold, their equipment only marginally suited for it.

Too close, and the heat from the landing thrusters could melt the surface ice, flooding and refreezing over any access points. They could seal the colony without ever setting foot inside it.

Neither option was acceptable.

Jo studied the terrain map, watching as potential landing zones appeared and disappeared with each new constraint layered over them.

Sensor spoke quietly.

"If I may make an observation."

He did not wait for permission.

"Any chosen landing zone will also be the departure zone."

The statement settled into the room with unexpected weight.

It was obvious, although no one had considered it.

Jo's eyes narrowed—not at Sensor, but at the realization itself--Simmons would have caught it. The map shifted again as the implications took hold. Several potential sites vanished from consideration immediately.

Keller exhaled slowly. Evan leaned forward, his earlier hesitation replaced by focus. Najma adjusted her stance, already recalculating.

No one spoke for several seconds.

They had arrived.

The system was in front of them. The colony was there, beneath the ice, waiting—whether it knew it or not.

And yet, beneath the calculations, beneath the planning and preparation, there was a quiet sense that something had not aligned the way it should have.

Jo could not name it.

She only knew it was there.

HONORA VI

Alta sat at one of many mending tables around the colony. The air carried a faint chill from the outer tunnels, and the stone beneath her feet held it. The evening walk was on, and she greeted others as they went past. At the entrance to the dining hall, she could watch the little ones and answer questions as people passed.

All the mending tables were organized the same way—so anyone could spend time at one and know exactly what was needed. A section for new items, a section for finished items, and in the middle was the workspace. The tables were worn smooth from years of use, the edges softened by hands that came and went.

A pair of dull garden shears caught her eye earlier in the day, she returned this evening to sharpen it. With shears in one hand and sharpening stone in the other, the clanging of the two echoed in the hall. The sound drew the attention of a little one on their walk with older kids.

Having peeled off from the group, the little one watched Alta's movements intently.

"What doing, eldermama?" The child stood back so as not to get hit with the stone.

"Ah hello, little one," she looked down from her work, greeting the child. "These shears were left for mending—"

"Who left?"

Alta chuckled at the inquisitiveness. "Not sure. Some people leave things, some people fix them. It doesn't matter who left it. We will fix it." The child readily accepted this answer. "I saw them earlier. A sharp stone will make them right again."

She demonstrated how the stone worked several times. Watching with delight, the little one's eyes widened whenever a spark flew. Noticing the interest, Alta pressed on.

"Mending is an important task for all of us to learn and help out. Do you want to try?" The child bounced happily and took the stone Alta held out for them.

Eager to try, the little one swung the stone at the blade and missed, sending the stone flying out of their hand. A pair of older children passed by and laughed softly at the mishap. Alta wagged her finger at them, but the child hadn't noticed, so no harm was done.

Scrambling to the floor, they picked up the stone and returned to the table to try again. Steadying themselves, the stone struck the blade. A spark flew in reward for their effort. The child laughed happily and gave the items back to Alta.

"Good work little one," she cheered, accepting the shears and stone. "When we help each other, we keep going. Now run along and catch up on your walk."

Smiling at the praise, the little one skipped off down the hall to find their companions.

Alta watched them go, counting without thinking. One more. Still here.

An earsplitting mechanical-sounding alarm filled the colony in the middle of the night.

Three of the Seven popped up in bed, hearts racing. For a moment they were too stunned to say anything.

"What—"

"Where—"

The questions overlapped, each reaching for a different edge of the problem.

The alarm was too loud for quiet voices. He rose from the floor bed and brought the lights up.

The sound did not change.

It was a warning.

Lio shielded her eyes, the sudden brightness sharp against the dark. Her hand moved instinctively to her belly. The muscle tightened beneath her palm.

She winced.

Breathed.

The third was already moving. She swung her legs over the edge of the bed and crossed the room, her hands finding clothing and tools without needing to see them clearly. Lio followed, slower but just as certain, gathering what they might need.

"What is it?" she asked, louder now.

Thia shook his head once.

"I do not know."

That was not a good answer.

There were not many things on Honora they did not know.

The alarm did not stop.

It did not pulse or shift or repeat in a pattern.

It simply *was*.

A constant, mechanical scream that pressed into the walls and through them.

Lio slung a bag over her shoulder, one hand still braced against her stomach.

"This is not the wind," she said.

"No," Thia agreed.

The winds spoke differently. They rose and fell. They moved through the tunnels like something alive.

This sound did not move.

It held.

They stepped into the corridor together.

Doors had opened along the hall. Others emerged, blinking into the light, hands already reaching for tasks without needing instruction.

No one asked who was in charge.

No one waited to be told what to do.

They looked.

They listened.

They moved.

"Where is it coming from?" Rosa asked.

Thia turned his head slightly, listening.

The sound carried through the stone, but not evenly.

"Central systems," he said, head cocking trying to locate a source.

"Or above."

That second possibility settled heavily between them.

Above was not a place that required attention.

Above was a place that was endured.

A little one cried somewhere down the corridor.

Rosa was already moving toward the sound.

"Stay," she said to Lio.

Lio shook her head.

"I am fine."

She was not.

But necessity existed.

Thia moved to her other side, simply adjusting to support her weight if needed.

They reached the junction.

Others had gathered there, faces turned upward, as if they could see through the rock.

The alarm pressed on.

Unchanging.

Unyielding.

"Has anyone heard this before?" someone asked.

No one answered.

Because no one had.

They must be old systems.

Installed long before them..

Maintained because Doc said:

If it is there, it has a purpose.

Thia stepped forward, scanning the wall where the access panel was known but not used.

"Open it," Lio said.

"It is already open," he replied.

That was not right.

The display flickered.

Numbers.

Symbols.

Ones they were taught, but did not use.

Rosa leaned in beside him.

"What does it say?"

Thia did not answer immediately.

He read it again.

And again.

As if repetition might change the meaning.

"It is a proximity alert," he said finally.

The words did not fit in the room.

"Proximity to what?" someone shouted.

Thia did not look away from the display.

"It does not say."

Lio felt the contraction build again, slower this time.

Deeper.

She breathed through it, eyes fixed on the panel.

"What is near us?" she asked.

No one answered.

Because there was only one thing that could be near them.

And it had never been near them before.

Above.

The alarm shifted.

Not in tone.

In meaning.

Once heard, it could not be unheard.

Something had arrived.

Rosa's hand tightened around Lio's.

"We stay together," Rosa said.

No one needed the reminder.

Still, it was said.

The alarm continued.

The colony did not stop.

People moved.

Little ones were gathered.

Tasks were assigned without words.

Lio exhaled slowly, her hand still resting over the lives she carried.

For the first time in many years, something had changed.

Not in the tunnels.

Not in the winds.
Not in the slow counting of their numbers.
Something had come to them.

CHAPTER 21

The search for the entrance to the Honoran colony took less time than anticipated.

It was not hidden.

There had been nothing to hide from.

The ice covering the outer doors was thick but not insurmountable. Terran cutting tools worked through it in steady, controlled passes, exposing metal beneath—scarred in places, fused along the seam.

Welded shut.

They had not expected to leave quickly.

That should have meant something to Jo.

It did.

Just not in time.

By the time they were inside, the temperature had stabilized, the air was breathable, and the corridors beyond the entrance lock did not look like an emergency shelter.

They looked lived in.

Not temporary.

Not failing.

Maintained.

That was the part she kept noticing without yet understanding.

The walls had been patched and repatched over time, but carefully. Air exchange systems were old, but quiet. Lighting was sparse, not broken. Nothing about the place suggested collapse. Not comfort, exactly. Not abundance.

But continuity.

And continuity, Jo had learned, could be misleading.

So she held to the frame she understood.

Medical screening and support if needed. Evacuation capacity. Temporary transport windows. Stabilization timelines.

She explained it all as clearly as she could, standing in a widened corridor space that was apparently used for receiving visitors, though she had no idea how often Honora actually had any.

Not often, presumably.

She spoke the way she had been trained to speak in crisis environments: calmly, precisely, with enough structure to reassure people before they knew what to ask.

When she finished, the silence that followed felt wrong.

No one moved.

No one reached for the supply cases stacked behind Evan and Keller.

No one asked how many people they could carry.

No one looked relieved.

The Honorans stood in a loose semicircle facing them, still and attentive. They were not shocked. Their patience unsettled Jo. It was as though they were waiting for Jo to realize she had said something unusable.

Finally, one of the women at the center spoke.

The words were almost entirely unintelligible. Almost.

"Ye cam onna Sinel."

Jo blinked.

"What?"

The woman repeated herself, slower this time.

"Ye cam... onna Sinel."

Jo caught *Signal* on the second pass, but nothing else. Beside her, Keller went still, listening intently with a trained ear.

Another Honoran—standing just off the first woman's shoulder—added something rapid and clipped.

Jo understood maybe one word in four. She looked at Keller expectantly, who answered with a head shake and small shoulder lift. She didn't know. That was worse than Jo not understanding--Keller usually understood language before anyone else realized there was a problem.

Keller took one step forward, brow furrowed.

"Wait," she said quietly. "No, I—hold on."

The first woman's gaze moved to her immediately. Keller tried again, slower, adjusting her own cadence by instinct. The woman answered at once. Keller frowned but forced herself back to a neutral expression.

A man near the back said something Jo couldn't catch at all.

Keller's expression shifted. She still didn't understand the words, but now she had a recognition of the scale of the problem.

"This isn't another language," she said, mostly to Jo now. "It's language drift. It's Terran, but—" She shook her head once, frustrated. "It moved farther than it should have."

"Than it should have?" Evan muttered under his breath.

She wanted to explain how it had flattened in some places, stretched in others. Consonants were dropped or softened. All of the familiar Terran language structures had been reduced to something faster and cleaner--and no longer naturally legible. But all that wouldn't mean anything to the team.

Jo looked back at the Honorans, suddenly aware of how badly the conversation had stalled.

This was first contact.

Actual first contact, after all this time, and she could not even tell whether the people in front of her had understood the difference between *evacuation* and *medical support*.

She hated that more than she had expected to.

Sam stepped forward before the silence could harden into failure. She did not move quickly.

She simply entered the space as though she had already been part of the conversation and was only now making that fact visible.

"The vowel shift is consistent," she said.

No one answered. Keller started to agree, but stopped, she didn't want to interrupt the tenuously restarted conversation. Sam tilted her head toward the Honorans.

Then, carefully, she said,

"Ye sent Sinel. Ask help."

The room changed, it wasn't dramatic, just enough to feel like progress.

The first woman's expression eased by a degree.

"Yes," she said, this time slow enough for Jo to understand. "Ask help."

Sensor moved beside Sam. "The syntax has compressed," he said. "And several root terms have narrowed in meaning. They are using a descendant dialect with significant isolation drift."

"That is not helping right now," Evan said.

"It is helping me," Keller snapped, still listening hard. She felt validated by the android's same recognition of the problem.

The smaller woman—the one who had spoken second—stepped forward eagerly and pointed to one of the supply crates.

"Meda? Seeda? Reprika?"

Sam looked at the crate, then back at Jo.

"She is asking whether we brought medicine, seeds, and a replicator."

Jo stared at her. "How did you—"

Sam did not look at her. "She has repeated the list three times," Sam said. "It is the most important part of the exchange so far. I could get a pattern to recognize"

The first woman said something else, slower now, with visible effort.

Sam listened. So did Sensor.

Keller closed her eyes briefly, as if trying to feel the grammar settle into place rather than solve it all at once.

Then her eyes opened again.

"Oh," she said, very softly. "Oh, damn."

"What?" Jo asked.

Keller looked at her.

"The language is... stripped. Efficient. If they sound abrupt, they're probably not being abrupt." She glanced back toward the Honorans. "They're speaking like every word costs something."

Jo looked at them again, and suddenly their stillness read differently. They were not passive.

Lio—because it had to be her, somehow; she had the gravity of center even before Jo knew her name—spoke again.

This time Sam answered first, in the drifted structure.

A short exchange passed between them. Quick. Clean. Exact.

Then Sam looked back at Jo.

"She says: you came because of the Signal."

Jo exhaled once, relieved enough to almost resent it.

"Yes," she said immediately. "You asked for help."

Sam translated—not word for word, Jo suspected, but by structure and sense.

Lio's attention shifted to Sam without hesitation.

Not because she understood more.

Because she felt less expectation to react appropriately.

Sam leaned in, listening once more.

Then Rosa—bright-eyed, almost smiling now that comprehension was beginning to hold—added another hopeful request.

"Books," Sam translated. "If we brought them."

"What?" Jo stared. There were books on the *Viga* but they're not rescue supplies. She stopped herself, because Lio was watching her carefully. The woman was not confused, or relieved. She was waiting.

Sensor stepped forward. "The Signal transmitted a request," he said. "Please send help."

His voice was neutral, exact. Because that was the message.

Sam stilled, considering his comment.

"The phrasing does not indicate relocation," she said.

Jo shook her head not liking this. "That's implied," she said. "If conditions are no longer sustainable—"

Sam translated.

Lio answered immediately with heightened emotion, and this time Jo caught enough of it to hear the refusal before Sam gave it shape.

"We did not ask to leave," Sam said. The sentence was simple. Quite clear and unambiguous, and still Jo found herself trying to locate the alternate meaning inside it.

Keller spoke before she could. "You live underground," she said, slower now, adjusting instinctively to the compressed rhythm. "On a frozen world. With limited resources. With—"

She stopped, because whatever she meant was too large and too visible to compress neatly into one sentence. The rescue team had torn into tunnels, braced against the cold, were still waiting to see the old systems.

The math of attrition could only stack against them.

Lio answered Keller directly.

"With care."

Sam did not need to translate that one.

The word landed strangely anyway.

Jo felt it, but did not understand it. She looked from Lio to the others and tried again.

"You're safe?"

Sam rendered it into the drifted dialect with only slight hesitation.

Rosa answered first, "As safe as any."

Lio stood more straight at the reply, shifting weight on one hip, rubbing a protruding belly.

Sensor spoke again, quieter this time.

"They are not expressing distress in the expected format."

Jo shot him a look sharp enough that under any other circumstances it would have ended the conversation.

It didn't because androids didn't have the same nonverbal vocabulary she did.

"They sent a distress message."

"The Signal indicates need," Sam said, her gaze moving between the two groups. "Not necessarily departure."

Jo turned back to Lio, trying to anchor the conversation somewhere firmer.

"You need assistance."

"Yes," Lio said.

"And you cannot sustain your current conditions."

This time, when Lio answered, Jo understood enough herself to hear the shape before Sam confirmed it.

"Not indefinitely."

Relief moved through Jo before she could stop it. There, finally, the mission could move forward.

"We can relocate you to a stable environment," she said. "There are multiple habitable stations with long-term capacity. Medical support, agricultural infrastructure, educational systems—"

Sam translated.

The response came from the man this time—Thia, Jo would later learn.

And even before Sam gave it back to her, Jo knew from the shape of the room that something had gone wrong.

"You think we are enduring something we do not want to."

Sam's translation was exact enough to hurt. The room went still. Jo's face grew hot. All at once she became aware of what she had not been seeing. The walls were clean. The systems were old, but maintained.

The air exchange did not rattle. She felt dizzy as she turned to survey the space more fully.

The Honorans were not panicked. They did not look like they had been waiting at the edge of collapse for rescue to finally arrive. They looked tired, worn, but not displaced from themselves.

They stood as strong as the pillars of ice the team passed to get here.

Jo swallowed.

"Then why send the Signal?"

This time, the silence lasted longer. The kind of silence that existed because everyone present understood the shape of the answer before it had been spoken. When Lio finally answered, her voice was quiet and measured.

And for the first time, Jo understood most of it before Sam repeated it.

"We were abandoned," Sam translated. "Our resources are at an end. We will die here. That much is certain."

Jo waited quietly triumphant, for the request. For the part where she imagined Lio said, *so take us with you.*

It did not come. Nothing in the room broke. Nothing collapsed. No one changed expression. If anything the Honorans seemed to stand closer together.

And somehow that was the thing that unsettled Jo most. There was no despair, no urgency.

Slowly, Jo felt the shape of the mission shift beneath her, her stomach flipping from the invisible drop of the floor from her feet. But no longer what she had called it.

The word rescue no longer fit cleanly inside it.

And for the first time since receiving the Signal, she wasn't sure that was a misunderstanding on their part.

Chapter 22

Rosa opened the heavy door to their room, panting harder than she liked. The creak of the metal made her flinch. She didn't want to wake Lio. She and some others had spent the day showing the newcomers around the colony—and answering their questions.

So many questions.

Once they all learned to understand each other, the Terrans seemed to talk non-stop. It was exhausting. At least the android people were quiet. Unusual but quiet.

She had worried about the door creaking for nothing. Lio and Thia were squaring off around the central table.

"I can—" she jerked a thumb towards the door.

"Stay." They both said. The pair turned to look at her, their motion formed a mirror image.

"Sister, please stay." Lio said softly.

Rosa walked up to the table and set her bag down, feeling relief in her shoulders. As was their custom, she waited to be brought into the conversation. It was a simple agreement that kept harmony in their marriage.

The other two tried speaking at the same time, and stopping to allow the other to go. This repeated a few times, creating awkward stutters in restarting the conversation. And still Rosa patiently gave them time to continue. She wished there were chairs at the table. Another custom, the table was for working as equals. She saw a collection of items waiting to be mended on it, set in two piles on either side. A pair of tiny socks caught her eye, she would get to them later.

Thia extended his hand to Lio, offering her to go first.

"The Terran's arrival has created a complication." Thia snorted, Lio ignored it. "In deciding where to deliver the twins."

Rosa paused, taking the measure of the conversation.

Thia added, "I am struggling to express my support." He exhaled heavily. "I don't want to tell her what to do. Only provide thoughtful weight to the available options."

"I see." Rosa said. "I am not needed for this conversation, loves. You two have all the necessary information between you. She picked up her bag and headed for the door, grabbing a shawl on the way out. Turning back to the pair she left them with an admonition, "be sure to decide before necessity decides for you."

The two looked at each other, unhappy, the decision still needing to be made.

✦ ✦ ✦

Lio sat on the edge of the bed, staring at the dresser. Hand me down clothes and cloth diapers were piled unevenly on top. She warmed seeing the dolls made from socks too worn to be repaired. A monkey and a bear sat back to back. Rosa was on the evening walk, Lio would ask if she knew how to make a bunny. Maybe.

"How can I go to the ship among strangers, and unfamiliar equipment? What about their microbes? Doc would not like this."

Thia sat down beside her, work gloves and mending needle in hand. He leaned against her shoulder momentarily reinforcing his physical presence.

"Doc would want you to be safe. The twins to be safe." She knew it was true.

"What about the Seven always stay together?" She shot at him, like a final round of debate.

"What about 'be smart'?" Lio snorted, and leaned against him. The solid feel of him held her together.

"I do not want to make this decision. Neither choice feels right. I have to get this right."

Thia kissed her temple lightly. "It is not a test. The only thing you have to do right is bring the twins home." He had that very serious *Thia is always right* tone, but she was not convinced.

Home? Where would home be now?

She didn't want to leave but wasn't sure that it was right to stay. They had a way to carry on outside of these frozen walls. Maybe not everything was meant to carry on.

✦ ✦ ✦

"Esteemed Seven," Jo said stiffly.

Evan whispered to Keller louder than intended, "but there's only six." She elbowed him in the ribs, telling him to be quiet. Lio narrowed her eyes at him, having heard the comment.

Ignoring the exchange next to her, Jo continued, "your colony is a testament to the will to survive and care for each other under extreme strain. The Terran government's dereliction of duty in not providing continued support and connection was wrong and inexcusable. We offer a sincere apology for this inaction. In addition, we extend an invitation to reunite with Terra and retake your place in her society." There were murmurs of assent among the Honorans gathered to hear her speak. The six in the front row, with an empty chair beside them, however, were silent.

"You will receive all the rights and benefits of our citizenry. We will initiate, at your approval, supply delivery, communication restoration, and personnel support. We will provide structural, engineering, scientific teams..." Lio and Thia did not hear the rest as they looked at each other with an alarmed expression.

The hidden book's words floated in Thia's mind, "they can never know." His hands involuntarily balled into fists.

Sensing a shift in her partners beside her, Rosa interrupted, "thank you for this thoughtful statement and offer of recompensation. I believe I can speak for the Seven regarding your generous offer. Our society has been closed to the outside for many generations. The introduction of new peoples, while not unwelcome, does present certain risks we must carefully consider."

A sigh went through the front rows as she continued.

"We cannot make any agreements on that matter today, or even guarantee an answer prior to your departure." The Terran crew looked at each other, saying nothing.

"Assuming your offers are not conditional on Terran personnel residing in our colony, we would like to begin collaboration on certain items you listed. Communication restoration, medical facility repairs and supplies are the first of our needs."

Jo was stunned. She didn't know what to say. Falling back on diplomatic protocols, she responded formally, "Thank you, Rosa. We acknowledge your terms and await a time to meet regarding the repairs to communications and medical."

CHAPTER 23

The basin paths behind the eastern growth terraces had no obvious hierarchy. That was the first thing Sensor disliked about them.

They curved where they should have run straight, narrowed without warning, divided and rejoined in patterns that suggested intention without ever resolving into anything as satisfying as design. Water moved through shallow channels cut between the stone—not fast enough to sound urgent, only enough to make the entire terrace system feel quietly in conversation with itself.

Sam stepped over one of the channels without looking down. Sensor noticed that too. He had been noticing many things about Sam lately that he would have preferred to categorize and dismiss. Honora did not seem interested in assisting him.

Lio was several paces ahead, carrying a shallow woven tray against one hip. She had not asked for help. She had also not refused it when Sam followed. That, apparently, was invitation enough.

Sensor had come because Sam had. This was not a strong operational rationale, but he had stopped requiring those from himself where she was concerned. The air here was cooler than the upper terraces, damp where the channels widened, carrying the scent of mineral water, leaf rot, and something faintly metallic beneath both.

Not unpleasant. Only... alive in a way Tau Station had never attempted to be.

Lio stepped onto a lower platform bordered by pale fronds and set the tray beside a stone trough fed by a narrow spill of water. Sam stopped at the edge of the platform, Sensor stopped beside her. Lio glanced back once—not at either of them specifically, only to confirm they were still there—then knelt and sorted the contents of the tray: cutting tools, bundled fiber, seed pods, a coil of cord.

She gave no explanation, nor instruction. Sensor folded his arms.

"I do not know what we are doing."

She did not look up. "Yes."

That was not useful. Sam stepped down onto the platform, careful but not hesitant. The stone was damp and worn smooth by repeated use. A second trough sat farther down, water moving through it in intervals—collecting, releasing, collecting again.

It was more rhythmic than mechanical. Lio trimmed the pale fronds with quick, practiced motions.

Sam crouched beside the tray. "Can I assist?"

Lio handed her the fiber bundle. That appeared to be yes. Sensor remained standing. He was aware this positioned him as unnecessary, and he did not appreciate that.

Sam watched Lio work briefly, then mirrored the motions—not precisely, but not clumsily either. Adjusting. Separating damaged growth from usable. Leaving the smallest shoots intact. Binding stems loosely and placing them along the dry edge.

No one instructed her, Lio did not correct her. Sensor found that increasingly irritating.

"You have not done this before," he said.

"No." Lio glanced once at Sam's hands, and kept working.

Still no correction. Sensor looked between them.

"There is no consistency of method."

"There is," Lio said. She did not elaborate.

Water released from the upper channel, filling the first trough before spilling into the second. Sam moved one bundle aside a moment before the overflow reached it. Lio lifted the tray at the same time, just enough to keep the lower edge dry. The motion between them was not mirrored, not coordinated. It was simply aligned.

Sensor crouched beside the trough. There was no visible indication before the release. No mechanical marker. No reliable shift in sound. He waited through the next cycle. Then reached for the fiber coil—too late. Water touched it before he could move it clear. It wasn't enough to damage, just enough to register.

Lio said nothing. Somehow that was worse to him. Sam continued working, unhurried, uncorrected, present in a way Sensor could not reduce to process. He watched the sequence repeat once more before understanding what unsettled him.

There was no lead. No follow. No visible exchange of decisions. Yet the work continued without interruption. It wasn't optimized or inefficient. The work was simply whole. A breeze lifted the edge of Sam's sleeve.

She looked up—toward the upper channels—and reached across the trough to move the seed pods farther back. A moment later, water released again—stronger this time, spilling wider across the stone. One pod would have gone in.

It did not.

Sensor stared at the channel, and then at Sam.

"How did you know?"

Sam blinked once, "I didn't."

Lio said, without looking up, "she did."

He did not like that. "That is not a meaningful distinction."

"No," Lio said. "It is simply one you do not like."

Her echo of his thoughts landed harder than expected.

For the first time since leaving Tau Station, Sensor felt—not excluded. It was worse, he was adjacent.

Close enough to witness, not close enough to join.

When Sam found him later near the lower access rise, he was still standing where he had stopped.

She stood beside him without speaking. After a while, he said, "You anticipated four changes in flow without measurable warning."

"Yes." Her tone was subtly exuberant, proud even.

"That is not explainable."

"No."

He waited, but she didn't continue. That irritated him enough to turn.

Sam's expression was calm, precise—not defensive, not evasive.

Finally, she said, "I do not think it was asking me to predict anything."

He needed more information. "Then what was it asking?"

She looked back toward the terraces. "I think it was asking whether I would keep interrupting."

Sensor said nothing, that answer was worse than the others. And because, against all preference, some part of him understood it immediately. They stood there a long time. Below them, unseen in stone and root and gravity, water continued moving where it always had.

Not waiting. Only responding. Sam took his hand, he squeezed hers in response.

CHAPTER 24

Lio regretted their decision to take the long way through the tunnels. The Terrans said they wanted to “see everything” and they had meant it. She thought tiring them out like over-excited children would give her a good night's rest. Thankfully Thia had taken Evan and Sensor to the workshops. That left her with Jospehine, Janelle, and the android Sam. Perhaps she could compare notes with him later on what was revealed during their guest’s time apart.

Alta and Rosa had taken to following—accompanying—her everywhere. She knew they were right to do it, but felt constrained at their constant presence.

“What is down this hall?” Sam asked, pointing at a nondescript section of wall. Rosa and Lio looked at each other in surprise. “If you are wondering, I detected a micro-change in air flow and pressure around the seals."

"We don't go down there," Lio said as if that settled the matter.

"Why?" The android was curious, so Rosa tried to answer her without giving too much away.

"Elders decided to restrict the area. To keep the rest of us safe."

"Thank you," Jo said, placing a hand lightly on Sam's arm steering her away from the wall.

"Your leaders did not feel the danger could be resolved?" Jo said as they continued on down the tunnel. She thought about the cry, the winds, the Signal. Whatever it was held a death grip on this planet.

"Necessity exists," Alta said. Rosa and Lio nodded solemnly.

Sensing there was nothing more coming, they walked on. Lio, Rosa, and Alta took the lead.

Jo released Sam who bounded up to the others. Keller slowed to allow them all to get several paces ahead. "They're hiding something," Keller whispered.

"Maybe, or they really don't know."

"Do you believe—" Keller was cut off by a guttural cry ahead of them.

The women sprung into action, running towards the Honorans. Hearing their pounding footsteps, Rosa turned and held her arms out palms up, "please," she said calmly, "wait here."

The cries of labor rattled through the hall.

Alta helped Lio down to the smooth stone floor, already moving with purpose. The pack was stripped from her shoulder and emptied without ceremony. Supplies scattered. Rosa's hands moved through them immediately, sorting, checking, counting.

"This is not how—" Lio grunted.

The contraction took the rest.

Alta rolled the pack beneath Lio's head. Not comfort. Position.

"Breathe," she said, though she knew Lio would. Jo and Keller glanced at each other in alarm. Looking on either side of Keller, Jo had lost track of Sam. She poked her head around and then spotted her. The android knelt beside Alta, arranging the spilled items, organizing the chaotic pile.

Behind them, Jo stood frozen.

She had been told to wait.

So she waited.

It was the wrong thing to do.

Rosa nudged her foot gingerly through the supplies, disrupting the organization Sam created. The woman whispered as she pointed at each of them as if checking off a list. Picking up on her intent, Keller stepped beside her, "Is anything wrong?"

"Not sure," she replied, not looking up. "Where's the communicator?" She asked no one in particular.

Lio thrust it above her head grunting. Rosa let out a grateful sigh and took it from her. Pressing an assortment of buttons on the device, someone said on the other side, "Are you back—"

"Ungh..."

"Lio? Twins? Twins!" Thia shouted as he went on. "I'll be right there! Where are you?"

Alta turned and looked up at Rosa from her spot on the floor. Her look questioning if they should say. Rosa shook her head once. There was no sense in hiding it.

"We're in the forward quadrant behind the gate.

""BEHIND—"

"Unghhhh," Lio grunted loudly to cut him off. Alta smirked at her creative intervention.

"I'm coming," Thia said and closed the communication.

Jo's hands flexed uselessly at her sides. On the ship, this would have been controlled. Sterile. Monitored. Predictable.

Here, there was none of that.

Only stone. Breath. Sound.

A body collided with her.

She stumbled forward as Thia rushed past, already moving, already needed.

Jo braced herself against Keller to keep from falling.

By the time he reached them, the first cry had already come.

Sharp.

Full.

Alive.

Relief broke through the group like a wave.

One down.

It did not last.

Lio did not settle.

Her breathing remained uneven, her hands clawing lightly at the stone beside her. Rosa watched closely now, counting without sound. Alta's hand rested on Lio's knee—not to soothe, but to hold her in place.

"It's all right," Alta said.

It was not.

But it needed to be.

Sam had not moved.

She knelt where she had been, hands still among the scattered tools.

She had not heard anything.

But something had changed.

The air shifted.

Not in movement—in structure.

Pressure redistributed along the corridor walls, subtle but measurable. The ambient hum of the station systems thinned, as if a layer had been removed.

Sam did not reach for a device.

There was nothing to measure.

Pattern did not require instrumentation.

It required alignment.

Her attention narrowed.

Not outward.

Inward.

Tracking.

Lio gasped.

"This one—" Rosa began.

Stopped.

Alta looked at her.

Rosa looked back.

A decision passed between them.

"Now," Alta said.

The contraction came.

Different.

Not stronger.

Clearer.

Lio cried out—not in pain, but in effort—and something moved through the corridor.

Not sound.

Not air.

Release.

Sam felt it resolve.

The pattern closed.

The second cry followed.

Softer.

Thinner.

Alive.

For a moment, no one moved.

Then everything did.

Rosa laughed and cried at once, Alta's shoulders dropped with the weight of completion, and Thia fell to his knees beside Lio as though the ground had given way beneath him.

Jo exhaled.

Only Sam remained still.

She looked down the corridor.

Toward the sealed wall.

Nothing moved.

Nothing sounded.

But something had been there.

And now—

It was gone. For a moment, Sam considered that something had been waiting.

The corridor settled into a strange calm after the second cry.

The first child quieted quickly, swaddled and pressed against Lio's chest. Rosa murmured to him—sounds without words, older than language.

The second lay in Rosa's arms.

Smaller.

Still.

Breathing. Just.

Jo stepped forward before she could stop herself.

"Is the second one—" she started to say, but hesitated.

Alive felt too obvious.

Healthy felt too clinical.

She chose neither.

"Is there a problem?"

No one answered her question.

Not directly.

Rosa adjusted the cloth around the smaller child.

"Lio needs quiet now," she said gently.

Alta's hands moved with practiced certainty, checking, settling, not searching.

"The timing was... particular," she added.

Thia did not look at Jo at all.

His attention remained fixed on Lio, on the children, on the moment as it existed—not as it might be evaluated.

Sam spoke last.

"Both are present."

Jo tried to clarify, "that's not what I—" She stopped, because it was, and it wasn't.

Keller shifted beside her.

"They're... okay, right?" she asked softly.

Alta did not look up.

"They are here," she said.

The distinction settled into the space between them.

Not resistance.

Not avoidance.

Something else.

Jo stepped back.

She realized, with a slow and uncomfortable clarity, that she had asked the wrong question.

No one spoke for a while.

Jo stood back, hands clasped in front of her, unsure where to put herself. Keller hovered near the wall, watching with an expression she would later struggle to describe—like witnessing a complex equation resolve itself.

Sam knelt where she was, still as a marker placed with intention. She watched the space between the twins more than the twins themselves.

Alta was the one who finally broke the silence.

"We should name them."

Lio was pale, damp with sweat, exhausted past the point of pretense. Thia looked at her, searching, but did not interrupt.

Alta waited. She always did.

Lio shifted the first child slightly, adjusting the cloth around his shoulders. He was solid. Warm. Present in a way that left no doubt.

"Rin," she said.

The word landed gently, like something set down rather than announced.

Rosa repeated it once under her breath. Thia closed his eyes.

Alta inclined her head.

"And the other?" she asked.

Lio's gaze moved to the smaller bundle in Rosa's arms. The baby's chest rose and fell, shallow but steady.

There was a longer pause this time.

Sam felt it—not as tension, but as alignment. Like waiting for the correct interval.

"Ora," Lio said.

The name did not settle the same way. It didn't need to.

For a moment, no one spoke. Even the twins were quiet, their breathing offset but connected, a rhythm not yet learned but already shared.

Keller swallowed. Her eyes were bright.

"They're beautiful," she said, her voice barely above a whisper.

No one disagreed.

No one affirmed it either.

Sam watched Rin's hand curl, fingers brushing the edge of Ora's wrap. A small, uncoordinated movement. Accidental. Necessary.

Signal.

Echo.

She understood without understanding how.

And she did not say it aloud.

The moment had resolved without her.

There was nothing left for her to do.

That should have been enough.

It wasn't.

Jo turned away.

Not from the birth—from her own helplessness.

Jo's fingers brushed the wall. The stone was cold.

Smooth.

Grooved.

History, worn into the surface by hands that had passed here long before her.

She traced the pattern absently.

Then stopped.

Air.

A faint current pressed against her fingertips.

Not from the corridor.

From the wall.

She leaned closer.

A seam.

Not visible. Not obvious. But there.

A seal.

If Sam hadn't said anything...

Jo pressed her palm flat against it, trying to understand the construction, the join, the—she pulled her hand back. No. They don't go there.

Keller looked around quickly for Jo, she wanted to talk. "What are you doing? Get back here." Keller whispered, her voice carrying in the otherwise empty tunnel behind her. The voice anchored here, Jo stepped away from the wall. She hurried back to join the group, but her mind was still at the wall.

Chapter 25

✦ ✦ ✦

"Your handling of the delivery was fascinating," Sam said to the eldermother she had come to know as Alta.

"Oh sweet child, Lio did all the work. We were there to remind her she could. And to catch the babies, of course."

"I am not a child." The eldermother looked over at her, "I am an android."

Alta laughed, "indeed you are. In a way though, we are all children, so long as we are learning and wondering."

Sam was quiet then. Was there not a difference between her learning and wonder, and a child's?

"May I confide in you Sam?" Alta asked quietly. She seemed subdued now. Not as youthful as after the twin's arrival. Sam's focus sharpened as she considered the question.

"You wish to tell me something you do not want to tell others?"

"That's right," Alta pulled her shawl close and turned to face Sam fully. "Will you keep my secret?"

Sam had never kept a secret. She had not shared information. But to have information that was not ever to be shared? Could she do it? Not tell Sensor? Not tell anyone? What if it was...

"I will keep your secret," she said decisively.

Alta nodded and released the breath she was holding. A small puff of white condensed as she did.

"I do not wish to leave," she said in a rush. Her shoulders lifted then as though a weight pressing her down had been removed.

Sam was unsure if this counted as secret information. Leave where? This nursery? The science facility? Oh.

"You do not wish to leave your home," Sam reflected back to her companion.

Alta looked tearful, but did not cry.

"You have only known this place. I understand. For hundreds of cycles I only lived on ten decks of Tau Station. I did not know anything or anywhere else existed."

The eldermother regarded Sam thoughtfully, not interrupting.

"Then the Signal from your people arrived. A small maintenance bot sent me on a journey to a new part of the station. So many others lived all around me, yet I had been alone." She took a breath.

"And then the Terrans arrived at our station. They asked to bring us here. To Honora. Before we left my... partner, Sensor asked if I was ready. I said 'no.' How could I be ready for something completely unknown? And still, we left.

Now I am here, with you. Every time I left behind what I knew—I did not like it."

Alta laughed softly, not expecting that remark in what seemed to be a pep talk from an android.

"But, like a child, I learned. And I felt wonder at new things.

"I will keep your secret eldermother Alta. And if you leave, I will be there to remind you there can be learning and wonder in new places."

Chapter 26

Jo had the crew meet on the shuttle, wanting distance from the colony before they made any decisions. The familiar hum of the systems should have been grounding. Instead, the enclosed space felt strangely uncertain now—as though the mission itself had slipped out from under them. Gathered around the data pad, the group considered their relocation plan. It would not be feasible to move in a single group. They could move them all to the ship by conserving their numbers use an around the clock schedule. Everyone would be boarded with their possessions in a day and a half. Keller played with a frayed edge of a shawl she didn't need. The material of their clothing protected them from the cold in the underground habitat. The worn shawl was a gift from one of the Eldermothers. She pointed at a spot between a surface hatch and the shuttle, "right about here, is a bottleneck that will make crates difficult to move. It will slow our progress."

Evan agreed with her assessment. "Could we bring a pulley to lift the crates in from above?"

Sam fidgeted beside Sensor. The secret she promised to keep for Alta was suddenly trying to burst out of her. Alta had not asked her to lie. Only to understand. Sam was discovering those were not the same thing. Silence could preserve a person, or erase them. She did not know which this would do.

I do not wish to leave. Alta's words replayed in her mind on a loop. Sam could barely focus on the rest of the conversation.

"It is worth considering," Sensor considered the potential of Evan's idea. His words brought her attention back.

"Let's discuss the—" Evan was cut off by Sam. She had to say something.

"I... I think we are not considering everything."

She didn't know how to proceed. The information she held was profoundly important, but the source required anonymity. This wasn't something she knew how to process. Not sharing meant being a participant in taking people from their homes. No one should do that or be forced into that situation of leaving. She knew the value of having one's own place to exist in peace. If she did tell the secret, then she's choosing for someone she cares about—and that choice they did not want to be made.

Sensor placed a hand on hers, "When you're ready, we are listening." The rest of the group looked on encouragingly, she must have been thinking for a long time.

"Not all the Honorans will choose survival over this place, their home."

"What do you—"

"—not all?"

"Who said—"

Sam had a memory of the council in Tau Station. She smiled recalling their lively debates.

"Who is not a relevant factor here," Sensor added helpfully.

"Yes, please understand," Sam said, looking directly at Jo. "There exist valid outcomes in which our assistance is declined."

"By assistance you mean rescue."

"Rescue implies danger. There's no danger here."

"They will all die."

"They will all die anyway. The population is too small. You heard Lio when we arrived—they know that."

"If we're not saving them, then why are we still here? Jo said defiantly. Her eyes went wide after hearing her own words. Her face fell and her eyes closed. The question had come from somewhere rawer than command. Jo hated that everyone had heard it.

"I... I... I didn't mean it like that."

Keller put her arm around Jo's shoulder. "We came here to help and now we're not sure what help even means." Jo sighed and sank into her friend's side.

"But they have to leave, right?" This place was not safe, she didn't care what any of them thought. "They can't stay here, can they?"

Sam looked over at Sensor, he was already looking at her. For a moment her problems fitting into the Terran team were gone. They were standing together to talk through the problem. "There is another option," Sam said looking back at the others. "When we first met the Honorans they said they sent the Signal because they had been abandoned. Not because they wanted to leave." She paused hoping they would reach the conclusion for themselves.

They didn't.

She found the Terrans often lacked the ability to see beyond their own ideas. They were on a search and rescue mission. But no one wanted to be rescued.

"So what do we do—just unload the ship and leave?" Evan asked. "How is that different from abandoning them all over again?"

"So we stay?" Jo asked not liking it. She felt like it was wrong, but still could not see the solution right in front of her.

"Evan is close to the point. Since Honorans asked for help and not rescue, and the system that brought them here also abandoned them—"

"Then maybe we stop treating them like evacuees," Keller said, leaning forward. "They're a colony. A functioning one—it doesn't matter that it's at an end state. If they asked for support, then maybe we support them like a colony."

Sam clapped, happy they were coming around to her vision. "Yes! We treat them like a colony. With an exchange of knowledge, and regular supplies. We give them an open channel of communication that should have existed all along."

Jo thought about her dreams. The winds that were not wind. She remembered the false wall in the tunnel. Leaving the people here under such strange conditions and an inhospitable environment felt wrong. A dereliction of her duty. But could she also forcibly remove them? No, she couldn't do that either.

Sometimes not doing wrong isn't the same as doing right. Commander Roger's words came flooding back to her. All of the choices felt wrong, but one had to be made. And duty, she realized, did not tell her which was which.

No one moved. They just looked at each other. No one looked relieved. The plan felt better than rescue, but not yet right.

"Okay, she said, "let's go tell them."

They returned to the shuttle in silence.

The answer was no.

The shuttle felt smaller on the way back.

No one sat where they had before. The air inside seemed stale, though Jo knew that was impossible. The meeting with the Seven had not been loud, or hostile, or even especially long. But it had left behind the kind of silence that changed the shape of a room.

"They said no. Were we expecting them to say no? I don't—" Evan's excited agitation was not something Jo felt prepared to wrangle at the moment. She scrubbed a hand through her hair and sighed.

"There's something not right here, and they know it," Jo said, more to herself than the others. "Why else would they want to keep our people out? We could help stabilize damaged areas. Secure access. Just that one false wall alone..." she trailed off, lost in thought.

Keller sighed internally, listening to Jo, thinking she might be missing the point.

"Well, Jo—Commander—if I may speak freely."

Jo allowed it.

Keller folded the shawl tighter around herself before continuing. "From what I'm hearing in your reasoning... they're right to slow this down. Listen to the words you're using. Stabilize. Secure. Access." She met Jo's eyes. "I think they could reasonably feel like they're going from being abandoned to being invaded." She shuddered, feeling an unexpected warmth flow through her. "That would make anyone worry, no matter how wrong we think things are here." It was undeniable that strange things, unexplainable things, had happened since they decoded the Signal—and it only got stranger since they arrived.

But was it right for them to push their way in, to... to what, research it? Attempt to contain it? They don't even know what it is, if it is anything at all. She wasn't totally sure they weren't just imagining it. And if the Honorans and the Seven were fine with it, she wasn't sure they should get involved at all.

Jo rubbed at her temple, visibly tired now. "What do you think?" Jo asked, turning to Sensor and Sam. They had been listening through the entire ceremony and this exchange, but hadn't said anything yet. The pair looked at each other, then back at the Terrans. Sam was quiet.

"I have noticed occasions where unexplained events occurred after our encounter with the Signal. They did not match any known patterns." She sensed that he spoke deliberately and also appeared careful not to look at Sam as he replied. Jo however, watched her the whole time. The android tilted her head at her companion's words, her eyebrows furrowed in a near identical human expression. Jo was beginning to think Sam was unaware of the oddities they had all seemed to experience. That in itself was odd. Sam had been quiet for so long Jo almost forgot she was there.

"We can't change them, we can only influence the conditions they live in," Sam said suddenly.

"Explain," Evan replied, curious how they could influence anything on Honora.

"Algae responds positively, or negatively to environmental stress. Maybe something about the planet is stressing them, and they don't even know it." Sensor tilted his head at her this time. Jo thought they were a rather compatible pair. "If we could figure it out—"

"But they don't even want us here." Evan interrupted.

"They don't want us in there," Jo said. "But they don't own the planet."

No one spoke for a long time. They milled about trying to occupy themselves unsuccessfully. It was as if being in the same room became unbearable. Evan and Keller left to find something to eat. Jo continued to wander around, looking at random objects before leaving as well. Perhaps she was giving her crew space before heading out. Being commander could be lonely sometimes.

Once Sam was sure the door had closed, she turned to Sensor. "I don't think I liked what they were implying," she said looking concerned.

"They seem to want to impose their will wherever they go." He replied, taking her hand in his. "Is there anything we can do?"

"We can try."

Neither of them said what trying might require.

✦ ✦ ✦

Lio and Rosa were spending time together talking through recent events; the new mother nursing one of the twins and her sister-wife folding blankets.

A red light started flashing next to the door. The two women looked at each other and Rosa set down her work. She grabbed the communicator on the dresser beside them and entered a sequence for Thia.

He answered already knowing what they were going to say, "Someone went behind the wall."

"Well, it wasn't any of us. All the little ones are in lessons. Do you think it was the woman?"

"She won't find anything," Lio said, touching Rin's cheek softly.

Thia was not impressed, "Yes, but she's looking. We can't trust her."

Rosa chimed in from beside Lio, "we are supposed to take her to the medical facility tomorrow."

Thia made an agreeing grunt, then said, "That's no good. She won't stop until she finds something." And closed the connection.

Chapter 27

Jo stood in the same stone tunnel where Lio had delivered the twins only days ago. Facing the false wall panel, she could barely distinguish it from the rock on either side. The concealment was deliberate. That much was obvious. What she still didn't understand was why, in a colony this small, something dangerous needed to be hidden instead of simply forbidden.

We don't go there, Lio had told her.

As though that explained anything.

She had brought several kinds of measurement sensors and toolkits to ease her way into the space beyond. Atmospheric sensors to detect pressure gradients. An electric multimeter to identify active current. Several others she knew were useful mostly because someone had once told her which buttons to press.

None told her the way through.

Jo's thoughts started to spread in multiple directions. If she allowed herself to get distracted she would miss something important. Pacing to calm herself, she ran her fingers along the wall as she did before. The cool rock soothed her.

She told herself she was there to gather information. If they were returning the Honorans to the Terran fold, reports would have to be made. Future teams would need something more useful than warnings and half-answers.

That was the official reason.

The less official one was that she had not been able to leave it alone.

Her pacing returned her to the false wall, feeling the air barely slip between the seam, she had no more idea what to do than before. So she sat down with her back to the panel, hoping time would bring an answer.

A pressure plate clicked beneath her. A slight shift at her back told Jo the panel had opened.

So clever.

She jumped up, and the false wall eased ajar without her weight to keep it sealed.

While it was barely a crack, she could slip in a finger, and then two into the space to widen it further. Jo pulled it just wide enough to wedge into the space beyond. *This is it.*

Her pulse quickened. A cold rush moved through her, sharpening everything. Closing her eyes, squeezed between wall and rock, she wanted to open them fresh on the secrets hidden beyond.

Planting her feet squarely on the other side of the Honoran's false wall, Jo opened her eyes. She scowled, as her first reaction was disappointment. The hall didn't look significantly different from the one she just left. She turned around to be sure she had actually changed places. The wall behind her was still open.

The lights were on, which was unusual since she didn't see any motion sensors. Maybe they were on all the time—not particularly energy efficient. The air was stale but just as breathable as the rest of the habitat.

As she progressed into the tunnel, Jo was careful not to touch the walls. Since this one was cordoned off—she didn't want to inadvertently touch something hazardous.

The evidence of their concern couldn't be too far ahead. Passing room after room, and multiple branching hallways, the only thing Jo thought was odd was how everything was clean. Most rooms were empty aside from built-in or large furnishings. The items left in other rooms were neatly organized as if someone could quickly get in and out with what they needed.

Not wanting to get lost, Jo stayed on the main walkway avoiding turns. Every step seemed to take her past more and more of the same clean, emptiness as the one before it.

She shook her head in confusion.

Pulling a multi-scanner from her bag, Jo retook measurements of the air. Nothing new. She scanned the walls, floor, and lighting panels. Nothing, nothing, and more nothing.

This can't be it.

She turned in a slow circle several times, looking for something, anything she missed. Dangers simply aren't... invisible.

Maybe I'm just not there yet.

She kept walking, and scanning. Checking every room, entering each one. Sometimes she moved crates around, sometimes not.

There was no dust. That unnerved her. If no one came here, why was it so clean?

Did she misunderstand?

Is this just... unused space?

She was annoyed wondering if all of this effort was for nothing.

Jo shook her head trying to clear it of the unwelcome thoughts. The Honorans wouldn't hide it if it wasn't dangerous to them.

That time she heard herself.

To *them.*

She remembered Lio's words about the wall, *some dangers must be avoided.*

The danger here was undetectable to her.

Not absent. Just not hers.

She was not native to this planet. They were. Whatever this place held, it was dangerous to the Honorans in a way she could neither measure nor inherit.

I shouldn't be here. She thought as a light flickered beside her.

Keller was right.

She was invading a place she had not been invited to enter.

Jo did not trust unmeasurable hazards. Safety, to her, had always been something that could be assessed externally. Risks for one were risks for all—usually.

This was not a usual case.

She expected danger to look like damage. This looked more like a cauterized wound, clean and empty.

Jo didn't quite run back to the false wall, but she didn't linger either. Her skin prickled with the urge to leave and the equally dangerous urge to stay. As she reached the end of the hall, the lights seemed brighter. Too bright. Like a spotlight pointed at her. She squinted against it, and pushed lightly on the false wall panel. Her shadow made the pressure plate lock momentarily visible. It was still open. She pushed it with her finger and felt it click into place.

Jo stared at the panel.

Then, very quietly, she said, "Damn."

Chapter 28

✦ ✦ ✦

"Najma?" Sam asked quietly. She walked over to where Najma was working on some manifests for transferring supplies from the ship.

"Yes, Sam?" Najma looked up from her datapad. Since coming to the colony, their interaction had been minimal. Najma accepted it as a change in environment, altering their relationship temporarily.

"I am... struggling here." Her volume dropped, hoping to convey a confidential nature to the conversation. "Nothing in this place fits known patterns for me."

"What have you noticed?" She gestured for Sam to sit beside her, and set the datapad on a workbench.

"Everything functions. But they function..." she trailed off, not sure how to describe the wrongness. Many descriptors scrolled through her language processing. Their definitions were close, but not accurate enough.

Najma was patient, giving Sam time. She seemed almost frozen, locked in thought. She did not think interrupting would produce a faster result.

Sensor walked into the bay designated for the android's workspace. As it was nearer to the surface, the temperature was uncomfortably low for humans. They were not asked if it was uncomfortably low for them.

He stopped just inside the doorway, eyebrows furrowing. His toolbox felt heavier all of a sudden so he set it down. Not wanting to disturb the scene in front of him, he took precaution to not move too quickly or with excess sound.

Before him, Najma and Sam sat facing each other—completely still. Could Sam's affliction be transmitted to others? He noticed a higher frequency since coming to the planet. Such a change would be deeply troubling.

Najma turned her head and acknowledged Sensor's entry. She beckoned him to join them. He waved her off and picked up his toolbox, noting that it now felt significantly lighter.

He gave the pair a wide berth, circling behind Sam to reach his workbench. Setting the toolbox down, he took a moment to consider what the increase to Sam's freezes might mean. For her. For them. For all of them.

"Synchronicity. This place constantly has nearly concurrent odd events and I find it disturbing." Sam said, suddenly finishing her sentence.

Najma began to reply, but stopped. That was not the ending she expected, or was even able to follow. The syntax change was completely confusing. Sensor pushed the tools around on the bench, still facing away from the two. He rattled some tools, making a familiar sound that would announce his presence to Sam.

She looked over her shoulder toward the clattering and brightened upon seeing him. "Come over, I think you need to hear this too." Sensor set his tools down and joined them.

"Can you provide examples of these "synchronicities" you have observed?" Najma asked. Still not that sure what the word event meant.

Sam folded her hands in her lap. It was not a defensive posture. It was containment.

"Yes."

She hesitated.

“I noticed them after the initial decoding of the Signal. At the time, I categorized them as statistical convergence.”

Sensor clocked the term, it was a familiar classification.

“Convergence of what?” he asked.

“Human reactions. Environmental shifts. My own processing.” She turned her gaze to Najma. “Individually, each occurrence fell within acceptable variance. Cumulatively, they do not.”

Najma leaned forward, engaged. “Describe one.”

Sam took a breath.

“When Commander Willis first entered the Honoran system, Evan Chen hesitated before making the announcement. His pause exceeded his baseline decisional latency by 0.8 seconds.”

“That is not significant,” Sensor said gently.

“Not alone,” Sam agreed. “At that same moment, Keller’s respiratory rate elevated without environmental stimulus. And I...” She stopped.

“You what?” Najma asked.

“I anticipated the hesitation.”

The room felt quieter.

“In what sense?” Sensor asked.

"I formed a response to a delay before the delay occurred."

Najma's eyebrows lifted.

"You predicted it?"

"No." Sam shook her head. "Prediction requires model input. I did not have sufficient data."

"Then what was it?" Sensor pressed.

"I experienced the expectation of delay."

She watched their faces carefully.

Najma spoke first. "Continue."

Sam inclined her head.

"Two cycles later, I thought of Alta. I was not scheduled to see her. I did not send a communication. She arrived within seconds."

"That can happen," Sensor said.

"Yes. It can." Sam's voice remained even. "But this has occurred repeatedly. Thought followed by encounter. Emotional spike followed by environmental fluctuation. Keller hears a cry. Alta hears wind. Their physiological responses diverge. Yet the timing aligns."

Najma's gaze sharpened. "You believe these events are linked?"

"I believe they are coupled."

Sensor stilled.

"That is not the term you used moments ago," he said quietly.

Sam looked at him.

"I was selecting vocabulary that would be accessible to Terrans."

Najma's lips twitched faintly. "And now?"

"Now I am selecting vocabulary that is accurate."

She shifted slightly, the smallest physical sign of discomfort.

"When I navigate the tunnels, I occasionally alter direction without conscious reasoning. Later, I discovered that an event occurred along the path I avoided."

Sensor replied too quickly.

"You did not register an input?"

"No."

"Not acoustic, thermal, electromagnetic?"

"No."

Najma considered this. "Could you have processed micro-variations subconsciously?"

"Yes." Sam paused. "But that would imply my internal systems are adapting to environmental signs without surfacing them to conscious layers."

Sensor's voice lowered. "Is that distressing?"

"Yes."

The word landed plainly.

Najma replied slowly. "Because you cannot model the interface."

"Correct."

He folded his hands. "Are these synchronicities impairing your functioning?"

"No."

"Altering it?"

Sam hesitated.

"Yes."

In the far corner of the bay, something metal contracted with a soft ping as the temperature shifted.

Najma spoke carefully. "On Tau Station, we existed in a closed system. Every variable had traceable origin."

"Yes," Sam agreed.

"This is not a closed system," Najma continued. "You may be experiencing environmental coupling."

"Coupling without a defined interface is unstable," Sam replied.

"Only if resisted," Najma said.

Sensor watched the two of them, then asked, "Do you believe the Honorans experience this coupling?"

Sam's gaze unfocused as she replayed recent interactions.

"They do not react to the same stimuli as the Terrans. Yet their reactions are coherent within themselves."

"Meaning?" Sensor prompted.

"They are not hearing something new." Sam's voice softened almost imperceptibly. "They are within it."

Najma inhaled slowly.

"And we," she said, "are brushing against it."

Silence settled.

Sensor studied Sam's expression.

"You are not malfunctioning," he said at last.

Sam looked at him.

"That was not my primary concern."

Najma did not respond right away. "What was?"

Sam's fingers flexed in her lap.

"What if this place is not producing coincidences," she said carefully, "but responding to contact?"

The words lingered.

Sensor's gaze shifted toward the rock wall of the bay.

"Then," he said slowly, "we must determine whether we are observers."

Najma finished the thought.

"Or participants."

The temperature in the room did not change.

But something in the space between them did.

And for the first time since arriving on Honora, Sam could not tell whether the pattern was forming around her—or through her.

Chapter 29

"Do you hear that?" Keller and Alta said at the same time. The women laughed, though it was mirthless and short-lived. They went back to their task sorting supplies from the Terran ship. Little ones ran through the maze of crates, enjoying the novelty. One of the smaller children paused mid-run, going completely still. Then they resumed as if nothing had happened.

"The winds were loud is all..." Alta trailed off, not finding it particularly noteworthy.

"Oh, I thought I heard one of the twins crying, or perhaps another baby." Keller's eyebrows furrowed at their different recollections.

"There are no other babies," Alta said, too quickly. She let a barely audible sigh escape.

Keller stopped working and set her crate down. Fixing the lid in place, she sat on it. Sitting on the floor or the worn cushions like the Honorans hurt her back after awhile.

"I—" she began, but Alta stopped her.

"It's alright Janelle. There was a time when we could have babies every cycle, their cries echoed through the halls. Now our women are too old, too young, or too tired start over."

Keller regarding Alta thoughtfully. As one of the oldest people remaining in the colony, her words carried the weight of their history. The Honorans chose to continue on as though they were not dying out. The care they took with every aspect of life would be beautiful if it didn't depress her. They did their best to stay alive, but it didn't feel like living.

"That's odd don't you think?" Keller said, thinking about the cry Alta didn't hear.

"Not having more babies?" The old woman said, confused by the question.

"No, I just meant—we both heard something, just not the same something. That's odd." Keller didn't like puzzles very much. Sound was a form of communication, her specialty. But what is the communication if two listeners don't hear it the same way? Is it a communication of a different type?

“I suppose it is,” Alta said dismissively, her hands dropping for a moment. She set the gardening tool down a little harder than intended. The metal clinking against the other trowels and picks. “Well these tools won’t sort themselves.” She said hinting for Keller to get back to work.

✦ ✦ ✦

Lio sat among the plethora of medical supplies delivered from the Terran ship. The abundance was overwhelming. She would need to pull help and ask those willing to switch from their regular duties to organize and shelve it all. And label. And learn the new replicator. And catalogue. And, and, and. It was too much.

Every muscle in her body was coiled and ready to strike an invisible enemy. She knew though, the tension was not for fighting. It was for holding everything together.

That’s all she knew.

Stay together.

Be smart.

Necessity exists.

Was it really wise to stay here?

To live in their own graves...

She knew the thoughts were morbid, but they were also fleeting. There was no way they would leave with the Terrans--not now. Not after...

Ora let out a thin squawking cry in the sling against her chest. She worried about him. Small—he's too small.

Reve was small.

Asha was small.

Even though death was the only true birthright of her people, she still fought against it.

She sometimes wondered who would be the last of them.

Now with Rin and Ora beside her, it broke her heart to think it might be either of them.

She leaned into the sling, pressing her lips to Ora's soft hair. "Not yet," she whispered.

Lina, her student and assistant medic, walked in carrying new medical texts. It interrupted her thoughts. Lio tightened the wrap and reached for the nearest crate. There was still work to do.

Chapter 30

The mission crew gathered in the shuttle's operations bay in uneasy silence. Jo directed them there, but no one had called a formal meeting. The room had simply filled as one person after another drifted in, drawn by the same unsettled feeling. The shuttle had become the only place on Honora that still felt Terran.

That had once been comforting. Now it felt increasingly like a room built to preserve a version of the mission that no longer existed.

Sam stood beside the central console with a datapad in her hands. A series of graphs glowed on the screen behind her. The colored lines pulsed faintly in the dim light of the bay.

Jo leaned against the edge of the table, arms crossed. Evan hovered beside a terminal pretending to read something. Keller sat on a crate, elbows on her knees, staring at the floor. Sensor stood just behind Sam, hands folded loosely behind his back.

Najma was the only one studying the display.

Sam cleared her throat.

"I have been comparing the anomalous events we have all observed since decoding the Signal."

Jo's face scrunched some. "You mean the... dreams. The sounds."

"And the environmental fluctuations," Sam replied. "Including deviations in expected Terran behavior."

Evan glanced up. "Behavioral anomalies?"

Sam turned her head toward him. "Your hesitation before announcing arrival in the Honoran system."

Evan blinked. "That was hardly—"

"It exceeded your baseline decision latency by point eight seconds," Sam said gently.

Evan closed his mouth.

Najma gestured toward the display. "Continue."

Sam expanded the projection. Several overlapping charts filled the screen.

"Each individual event falls within acceptable statistical variance," she said. "However, when viewed cumulatively, a pattern emerges."

Sensor faced her more fully.

"What pattern?" Jo asked.

Sam touched the screen. The graphs shifted into a heat map of red pulses scattered across a rough diagram of the Honoran tunnels and surface structures.

"These markers represent moments when one or more Terran personnel reported perceptual anomalies."

Keller shifted on the crate.

"You mean the cry," she said quietly.

"Yes," Sam said as a mere formality.

"The amplitude and frequency of these events increase significantly when Terran personnel occupy shared Honoran space."

Jo straightened.

"That doesn't mean we're causing it."

"Correct," Sam said immediately. "Correlation does not imply causation."

Evan gestured at the screen. "The Honorans have lived here for generations. If something like this were triggered by presence, it would have destabilized them long ago."

Sam paused.

"They are immersed in it," she said. "We are discontinuity." The room went still, as the word hung in the air.

Najma leaned closer to the display.

"Explain," she said.

Sam isolated another set of data points.

"Honoran-only gatherings show no measurable increase in anomaly frequency. Android-only environments show minimal fluctuation."

Sensor spoke quietly.

"But mixed environments?"

Sam highlighted several clusters.

"The highest readings occur when Terrans and Honorans occupy the same space."

No one spoke.

Keller rubbed her hands together slowly.

"It gets louder when we're together," she said.

Her voice was almost embarrassed.

Jo stared at the heat map.

Sam layered another projection over the first: a time-lapse sequence of the red pulses spreading across the diagram. They started faintly, then gradually intensified.

Evan leaned closer.

"When does it spike?"

Sam scrolled the timeline.

The pulses brightened sharply at several moments.

Their arrival.

The decoding of the Signal.

Joint gatherings in the tunnels.

And then—

Jo's eyes narrowed.

"Stop."

Sam paused the display.

Jo stepped forward.

"Back up a few minutes."

Sam obeyed.

The spikes grew again.

Then peaked at a single moment.

Jo recognized the timestamp before Sam finished speaking.

Her stomach dropped.

She knew exactly where she had been.

She folded her arms.

"We are the only new element in the system," she said quietly.

No one corrected her.

Evan looked pale.

"So what are we doing?" he asked. "Agitating it?"

Najma shook her head slowly.

"Coupled systems react to foreign oscillations."

Sensor attempted to diffuse the tension.

"Not maliciously," he said. "Naturally."

Sam watched Jo instead of the display. "The current pattern is consistent with interference." The mission commander was slow to respond, as though it cost her something to say what came next. "We came because they asked for help."

"If we leave now, what exactly are we saying that means?"

Silence settled over the room.

Jo stared at the display for a long time. She had a feeling of deja vu—this same sense on Tau Station. Of being in the wrong place. Of being the variable in the experiment. If they left, she didn't know what was left of what they had come to do.

Finally she spoke.

"If we are the variable..."

Her voice dropped almost to a whisper.

No one answered immediately.

Because the logic was sound.

And because no one in the room liked what it required.

"...then we remove the variable."

Sam moved a step closer to Sensor. There was no satisfaction in being right. They had identified a pattern, not solved it.

No one argued with Jo's conclusion.

Keller looked up first.

"And if nothing changes?"

Jo exhaled slowly.

"Then we know it was never about us."

That possibility did not comfort anyone.

Keller shifted uncomfortably in her seat. "I was afraid this was true, and I hate that it is."

Evan rubbed the back of his neck.

"So... we just leave?"

Jo studied the glowing red pulses on the screen.

The system reacting to their presence.

The Honorans living inside something they barely understood.

The Terrans stumbling through it.

"Yes," she said at last. "We are done here," she said at last. "I know it's not what we came for. But we're done." Several of them nodded solemnly.

"We leave." Her voice was stronger, and more resolved. It was the right decision.

One of the NCOs slipped quietly into the hall. Several others followed.

Soon only Jo, Evan, and Keller remained in the bay.

No one spoke.

Evan met Keller's eyes and motioned toward the door. She stood quickly, ready to leave.

Jo didn't turn around.

By the time the bay was empty, she was still staring at the red pulse marking the moment she had crossed the wall.

Chapter 31

The council room was full again.

It had been full many times since the Terrans arrived, but the atmosphere felt different now. Quieter. Less curious. The novelty of visitors had worn away, leaving something more cautious behind.

The Seven sat at the long stone table at the front of the room. Six figures occupied their usual places, with the seventh chair remaining empty beside them.

The joint Epsilon-Tau mission crew stood together across from them.

Jo had insisted they all attend.

Evan shifted his weight from one foot to the other. Keller stood beside him, hands clasped tightly behind her back. Sam and Sensor stood offset from the others, their posture calm and composed in a way that made the Terrans look even more restless.

Rosa regarded them steadily.

"You asked for this meeting," she said.

Jo nodded.

"Yes. Thank you for agreeing to speak with us again."

Her voice sounded steadier than she felt.

Thia leaned back slightly in his chair, watching her carefully. Lio sat beside him, one hand resting lightly on the sling across her chest where Ora slept. Rin was tucked against Rosa's shoulder.

The room smelled faintly of warm milk and minerals.

Jo took a breath.

"When we arrived on Honora," she paused, "we believed we understood why the Signal was sent."

She paused.

"That belief shaped many of our decisions."

No one interrupted.

"We thought you needed... wanted rescue."

Thia's mouth twitched faintly, but he said nothing.

Jo continued.

"It has become clear that we did not understand what you were asking for."

The silence deepened.

Evan stared at the floor.

"We also believe," Jo said carefully, "that our presence may be influencing events here in ways we do not fully understand."

Rosa sat straighter then.

"Influencing?"

"Yes," Jo said.

She didn't elaborate.

For a moment, it seemed as though Rosa might press the point. Instead she simply folded her hands on the table.

"And what conclusion have you reached?" she asked.

Jo glanced briefly at her crew.

Then she faced the Seven again.

"We will be departing Honora."

A ripple moved through the room behind the Seven. Not surprise—more like a shift in weight. A held breath finally released.

The six at the table did not react immediately.

Lio studied Jo's face for a long moment.

"You have decided this," she said.

It was not a question.

"Yes."

Thia leaned forward, toward an invisible threat.

"Because we declined your invitation to leave with you?"

"No," Jo said quickly.

"Then why?"

Jo hesitated.

Because I crossed a line. Because we don't understand what this place is. Because we might be making it worse.

But none of those words would help now.

"Because," she said slowly, "we believe our presence is affecting things here in ways we do not understand."

Thia's eyebrows lifted faintly.

Rosa glanced briefly at Lio.

"And yet you still wish to help us."

"If you will allow it."

"What kind of help?" Rosa asked.

"The kind you asked for."

Jo gestured around at the tunnels and stone.

"Repair of the communication systems. Medical equipment and supplies. Technical manuals and spare parts for the replicator units." This process had long begun but she wanted to emphasize that this was all they intended to do... for now.

Rosa listened without interrupting.

"No Terran personnel will remain on the planet," Jo added. "What we leave behind will be tools, not oversight."

The words seemed to settle into the stone walls.

Lio shifted Rin on her shoulder.

"That is acceptable," she said quietly.

Jo hadn't realized how tightly she had been holding her breath until that moment.

Rosa inclined her head.

"Then we accept your offer of assistance."

She paused.

"But understand something, Josephine."

Jo met her eyes.

"We did not ask to be saved," Rosa said.

"I know."

Rosa studied her a moment longer, as if deciding whether she believed that answer.

Finally she replied, it was not with warmth.

"Then we will work together until your departure."

Jo exhaled slowly.

"Thank you."

The meeting dissolved after that. The crowd dispersed through the tunnels, voices low and thoughtful.

The Seven remained seated.

As the Terrans turned to leave, Lio spoke again.

"Josephine.."

Jo stopped.

"Yes?"

Lio's gaze was steady.

"You came a very long way to help people you did not know."

Jo said nothing.

Lio adjusted the sling gently, settling the sleeping infant against her chest.

"That was noble," she said softly, "if there are others, go with the understanding that your idea of help may not be what is required."

Jo appeared somber. There was nothing else to say.

Lio watched them go.

Behind Jo, Evan let out a quiet breath.

"Well," he murmured, "that could have gone worse."

Sensor's eyes flicked briefly toward the stone walls around them.

"Statistically speaking," he said, "that outcome remains possible."

Sam laughed, even though it felt wrong to do. "Indeed."

And somewhere deep in the tunnels, the wind moved softly through the rock.

✦ ✦ ✦

They sat together in the ship's common space, too quiet, too tired. The ship felt emptier than it should. They were bringing less back to Epsilon rather than more.

Evan broke first.

"So," he said, forcing lightness, "who do we help next?"

There was a laugh.

It came out wrong. Too sharp. Too desperate.

Someone snorted. Keller wiped at her eyes and shook her head. Jo leaned back and closed her eyes.

For a moment, relief moved through the room.

They were still themselves.

They could still laugh.

Then it passed.

Because no one answered.

Because the question no longer made sense.

"We didn't rescue anyone," Evan said finally, quieter now.

"No," Keller replied. "We didn't."

"But we helped," he said, though it sounded more like a question.

Jo opened her eyes and stared at the ceiling. "Did we?"

No one rushed to answer her.

Jo stared at the ceiling.

They had not rescued anyone.

If anything, they had arrived too late to save, too early to understand, and just in time to witness something none of them could explain.

And perhaps worse—they still did not know why Honora had been the first voice to break the silence.

Later, when the ship had gone quiet, Jo stood alone at the observation window.

Honora had already become small against the black.

From this distance, it looked motionless. Silent. Just another frozen world at the edge of a system no one had cared to remember.

She pressed her hand lightly to the glass.

Below, beneath the ice and rock, people she had not understood would continue on without her. Jo stared until the planet that had called to them was only a pale blue-white point against the stars.

Then even that was gone.

And somewhere in that frozen dark, something had answered.

Not them.

Something else.

✦ ✦ ✦

THE END

✦ ✦ ✦

CODA

The colony felt different after the Terrans left.

Not quieter.

Just... returned.

Their footsteps were gone. Their voices. The odd timing of them moving through spaces not made for them. It had been less than a full cycle, but already the tunnels seemed to have drawn back around the absence they left behind. The air moved easier. The lights no longer hesitated before brightening. Even the walls felt less watched.

Lio should have been asleep.

Instead, she stood in the med center with Ora tucked against her shoulder, warm and stubborn in the wrap. Rin had settled hours ago, heavy and content in Rosa's arms. Ora had not. He had eaten, complained, slept for twelve breaths, and woken again insulted by the arrangement.

She respected it.

She shifted her weight carefully and winced at the pull in her hips. Her body still didn't feel like it belonged entirely to her. Too loose in some places. Too tight in others. Her bones had not yet forgiven her.

Ora made a soft, offended sound against her neck.

"Yes," Lio murmured. "I know. Existing is difficult."

The baby huffed once and quieted.

Across the room, Rosa looked up from where she sat with one boot off and the other half unlaced. "If you wake him, you keep him."

Lio's mouth twisted. "Rude."

"Truth."

It was late enough that even the colony's necessary sounds had thinned. Water in the old pipes. The low breath of the air exchangers. Somewhere deeper, metal settling against metal with a soft knock.

Familiar.

That was what Lio had been listening for all evening. Familiar things. Familiar strain in familiar places. The colony had always spoken, if one knew how to hear it. It creaked. Breathed. Complained. Endured. It had rhythms. Predictable failures. Predictable recoveries. A life they had learned well enough to keep.

Ora shifted again, restless in sleep.

Lio adjusted her wrap and stepped into the corridor.

The stone still held little warmth from the day cycle. Lights brightened overhead as she moved, then dimmed behind her in patient sequence. Her free hand found the wall without thought, fingers sliding into the shallow worn places carved there long before she was born.

The mother she had never known had used them.

Doc had too.

The thought came and stayed.

Lio swallowed around it and kept walking.

At the bend toward the lower levels, the air changed.

Not enough to hear.

Enough to feel.

She stopped.

Ora made a small sound and buried himself more firmly against Lio's shirt. Ahead, the corridor looked the same as it always had. Same stone. Same light. Same narrow turn leading deeper into the colony.

But the pressure along Lio's skin had shifted.

A faint pull.

Then release.

Her breath caught.

Not from fear.

From recognition.

For one impossible instant, the old wrongness moved through her so cleanly that she was not in the corridor anymore but outside, cold biting through her clothes, darkness stretching endless beyond the colony lights. A child too small to understand why the wall had wanted her more than the world did. Reve laughing once and then not again. Doc shouting her name into the night. The unbearable silence after.

Lio gripped the wall so hard her knuckles hurt.

Ora stirred.

The corridor stayed still.

No alarm. No sound. No visible change.

Only that lingering sense that something had shifted where no shift should have been possible.

From behind her, Rosa's voice came softly from the med center doorway. "Lio?"

"I know," Lio said, though Rosa had not asked a question.

She didn't turn right away.

Her gaze stayed fixed on the bend in the corridor.

For one interminable moment, she had the strange and certain feeling that something beyond the stone had paused too.

Not watching.

Not waiting.

Only aware.

Ora fussed, small and immediate and alive.

The feeling broke.

Lio exhaled slowly and adjusted the baby higher, one hand steady at the back of his head. Whatever had moved—or almost moved—did not announce itself twice.

Behind her, Rosa waited without pressing. She had always been good at that.

Lio turned back toward the med center.

By morning there would be filters to change, nutrient slurry to check, and two infants to keep alive in a world that did not make easy promises. The colony would need what it had always needed.

Hands.

Time.

Endurance.

She took two steps, then stopped once more and looked back down the corridor.

The lights held steady.

The air did not move again.

Still, she found herself listening as she walked away.

As though Honora, having been answered at last, had not finished answering.

A Note on the Science

The science in this book is inspired by real questions in communication, biology, systems theory, cognition, and planetary survival. As with the first book, these ideas are not meant as instruction, but as foundations — lenses through which the story takes shape.

If *Tau Station* was interested in the problem of distance, this book is more interested in the problem of interpretation.

How do you know when something is really a signal?

How do isolated systems change over time?

And how often does the simple act of observing something change it?

You do not need a scientific background to enjoy the story, but if you're curious, the following sections offer a little context for some of the ideas moving underneath it.

✦ ✦ ✦

The Fermi Paradox

The Fermi Paradox begins with a deceptively simple question:

If the universe is so vast, and life seems possible in so many places... why haven't we heard from anyone else?

There are countless possible answers. Maybe intelligent life is rare. Maybe civilizations do not survive long enough to overlap. Maybe distance is too great, or time too unforgiving. Maybe everyone is listening and no one knows how to answer.

In *Tau Station*, I was interested in the silence itself — the scale of it, the loneliness of it, and the ways people shape themselves around unanswered questions.

This book is interested in a slightly different possibility:

What if the problem is not silence?

What if the problem is recognition?

A signal can exist and still be misunderstood. A message can arrive and still fail. Contact can happen and still not mean what the receiver thinks it means. Even if life is out there, overlap is not the same thing as understanding.

The Fermi Paradox is often framed as a question of absence.

This book is more interested in what happens when absence turns out not to be absence at all.

✦ ✦ ✦

Signals, Noise, and Pattern Recognition

One of the central scientific questions in this story is deceptively simple:

How do you know when something is truly a signal — and not just noise?

In real science, pattern recognition is both incredibly useful and deeply risky. We rely on it constantly. It helps us detect disease, identify stars and planets, decode communication, build machine learning systems, and make sense of incomplete data.

It also gets us into trouble.

Humans are very good at finding patterns. Sometimes we are right. Sometimes we are connecting dots that do not belong together. The more incomplete the information, the easier it becomes to mistake interpretation for certainty.

That tension sits at the center of a lot of scientific work.

In this book, the question is not just whether a signal exists.

It is whether the people receiving it understand what they are actually looking at.

✦ ✦ ✦

Closed Systems and Drift

Isolated systems do not stay still.

That is true of ecosystems, cultures, languages, social structures, and even the assumptions people make about what is "normal." When a group is separated long enough — by distance, disaster, or necessity — it does not remain a preserved version of what it once was. It changes.

Sometimes slowly. Sometimes beyond easy recognition.

Language drift is one of the clearest examples. Over time, speech changes. Meaning shifts. Familiar words become strange. But the same thing happens socially and structurally too. Communities adapt to the conditions they are living in, not the ones they came from.

That adaptation is not inherently tragic.

It can be painful. It can be strange. It can be hard for outsiders to understand. But change inside a closed system is not automatically damage.

That idea matters a lot in this book.

There is often an assumption in science fiction that rediscovery means recovery — that if one branch of humanity finds another, reunion should naturally restore what was "lost."

Real systems are rarely that obedient.

✦ ✦ ✦

Observation Is Not Neutral

This may be the scientific idea most central to the book:

Observation is not neutral.

In physics, the observer effect is often described very specifically — measuring a system can influence what is being measured. But the broader idea shows up everywhere.

Ecologists know that introducing a new species can destabilize an environment. Doctors know that intervention always carries unintended effects. Social scientists know that people behave differently when they know they are being studied. Engineers know that adding a new process or control to a system changes how that system behaves.

Even trying to help changes things.

The assumption that we can enter a system, examine it, and leave it untouched is one of the most persistent fantasies in both science and human behavior.

This book is very interested in what happens when that fantasy fails.

✦ ✦ ✦

Artificial Intelligence, Social Learning, and Emergent Behavior

The androids in this story are speculative, but the questions behind them are very real.

How does intelligence become social?

What happens when a system designed for function begins to develop preference, humor, attachment, ritual, or selfhood?

In current AI and robotics work, there is growing recognition that intelligence is not only about problem-solving or task completion. It is also about context, feedback, embodiment, memory, and interaction. Systems learn not only from information, but from environments and relationships.

That idea is pushed further in this book.

The androids here are not meant to be a prediction of where current technology is definitely headed. They are a narrative exploration of what might happen if intelligence were allowed to become communal, adaptive, and meaning-making in ways we do not fully control.

Which is another way of saying: interpretation matters here too.

✦ ✦ ✦

What This Book Does Not Explain

There are elements in this story that are not fully explained.

That is intentional.

Not because explanation does not matter, but because incomplete understanding is one of the most honest scientific conditions there is. In real research, people often work with partial models, provisional theories, and data that refuses to fit neatly into the frameworks available to them.

Sometimes the most honest answer is not certainty.

Sometimes the most honest answer is to admit that the system is larger, older, stranger, or more interconnected than you first believed.

Science is not just a collection of answers.

It is also a discipline of humility.

This book lives there.

About the Author

Meredith McCray writes science fiction focused on quiet systems, long distances, and the people — human and otherwise — who maintain them.

Her work explores communication, responsibility, and the spaces between intention and outcome.

She lives on Earth, and continues to believe that listening matters.

✦ ✦ ✦

What Comes Next

The Signal, picks up where *Tau Station* left off. It explores what happens after something is heard — and what it means to decide whether, and how, to answer.

Future stories in this universe follow distant colonies, the era known as the Healing, and the long consequences of choices made in the name of protection, progress, and survival.

All of these stories comprise the The Great Silence Universe.

✦ ✦ ✦

Books in The Great Silence Universe

<u>The Signal Series</u>
Tau Station
The Signal - coming soon
Return to Epsilon Station - coming late 2026

The Reckoning (working title) – coming later 2026

✦ ✦ ✦

The Honora Series
The Healing Series

www.ingramcontent.com/pod-product-compliance
Lightning Source LLC
LaVergne TN
LVHW100513110826
845146LV00002B/627

* 9 7 9 8 9 9 4 4 8 5 1 2 5 *